From award-winning author Jean Gill: including Winner of the Global Ebook Award for Historical Fiction, IPPY award-winner, twice finalist in the Wishing Shelf Awards, Historical Novel Society Editor's Choice, and finalist in The Chaucer Awards. *Left Out*, Book 1 of the series *Looking for Normal*, was short-listed for the Cinnamon Press Novella Award.

PRAISE

"A compelling story about friendship, its strength, and the unusual ways it develops."
REBECCA P. MCCRAY, *THE JOURNEY OF THE MARKED*

"A must for all left handers." AGL REVIEW

"Jean Gill brings her magical storytelling skills to teens, to weave compelling and thought-provoking stories that will linger on in their minds well after the last page is read."
KRISTIN GLEESON, AUTHOR AND CHILDREN'S LIBRARIAN

"I would most definitely recommend this book to a friend because it is very interesting."
SHAELAN SCOTT, TEEN TURF REVIEWER FOR *READERS REVIEW ROOM*

"This book was a short interesting read. It really moved me with how people will do every little thing they can to make what they believe get across to others."
CHARITY MARTINEZ, TEEN REVIEWER FOR *5 GIRLS BOOK REVIEWS*

BOOKS BY JEAN GILL

Looking for Normal (teen fiction/fact)
Book 1 Left Out *(The 13th Sign)* 2017
Book 2 Fortune Kookie *(The 13th Sign)* 2017

Novels
Someone to Look Up To: a dog's search for love and understanding
(The 13th Sign) 2016

The Troubadours Quartet
Book 3 Plaint for Provence *(The 13th Sign)* 2015
Book 2 Bladesong *(The 13th Sign)* 2015
Book 1 Song at Dawn *(The 13th Sign)* 2015

Love Heals
Book 2 More Than One Kind *(The 13th Sign)*2016
Book 1 No Bed of Roses *(The 13th Sign)* 2016

Non-fiction/Memoir/Travel
How Blue is my Valley *(The 13th Sign)* 2016
A Small Cheese in Provence *(The 13th Sign)* 2016
Faithful through Hard Times *(lulu)* 2008
4.5 Years – war memoir by David Taylor *(lulu)* 2008

Short Stories and Poetry
One Sixth of a Gill *(The 13th Sign)* 2014
From Bed-time On *(National Poetry Foundation)* 1996
With Double Blade *(National Poetry Foundation)* 1988

Translation (from French)
The Last Love of Edith Piaf – Christie Laume *(Archipel)* 2014
A Pup in Your Life – Michel Hasbrouck *(Souvenir Press)* 2008
Gentle Dog Training – Michel Hasbrouck *(Souvenir Press)* 2008

ISBN 979-10-96459-03-2
Cover and interior design by Jessica Bell
Cover and interior images © moypapaboris, kotoffei, Gorbash Varvara, Crystal Home, Panda Vector

FORTUNE KOOKIE

JEAN GILL

FOR THE TWO PRINCESSES E**** IN MY LIFE
WHO CAN BOTH BE FOUND IN

Kidwelly

one by name
and one who dwells by the castle

CHAPTER 1

"You're not serious?" Ryan grabbed his friend's arm so he could stop her walking and check her expression but there was no hint of fun in the clear blue of her eyes. "No one's mother could be that stupid, especially yours."

Jamie shook her head. "At first I thought she was doing it for a laugh, but she was on the phone for hours so I had a look at the bill. She keeps all that stuff so tidy in a drawer and Dad never goes there. And it was all there, sometimes she's calling every day, and not just this month, neither."

"So, what are we going to do about it?" Ryan's whole face wrinkled up as he considered the problem and he missed the grateful look that came his way.

"I have this idea," she admitted, "but I need help."

"That's enough gossip, you two – you're late," Mr Jones pointed out, tapping his watch as he ushered the tail end of a queue into the Science Lab.

"Why do they do that?" muttered Ryan, "as if we're foreigners who need pictures to go with the words or something."

"It's in their training," replied Jamie under her breath, as Ryan flashed his teeth widely at Mr Jones.

"Sorry Sir," he said, "we were checking the weather

station, and we got into discussion over whether there was any connection between climate change and the planet's magnetic fields."

The teacher's eyes lit up with the inner glow of too-rarely indulged obsession. "Funny you should say that," he began, waving vaguely at the rest of the class to sit down, and frowning at three restless characters doomed to the front bench for previous misbehaviours. "There is a very exciting documentary coming up on TV…"

Jamie let the teacher-speak wash over her. She was used to this situation from hanging around with Ryan, and the important thing was that she'd managed to talk to him, and that something was going to happen. That, too, was not unusual with Ryan.

For the tenth time, Ryan said, "I just can't believe it. Now if it was my mother–" he broke off and they listened to Mrs Anderson bashing away on a laptop, occasionally coming out with a, "Goddam" or, more obscurely, "bill of rights mean nothing to you guys?"

Ryan's mother was a journalist who still kept her American links although she lived in Wales now. She'd lived there long enough to stop calling it 'Wales, England', but she still found ways to embarrass her son.

To give his mother her due, she would have been an embarrassment anywhere, as Ryan often said,. He could not understand that Jamie was a little in awe of Mrs Anderson's glamour, her southern States accent and the way she talked about her book on the federal states of Europe, as if writing such a thing was normal parent behaviour – as if writing anything was normal.

Knowing, as Jamie did, that Ryan's mother had "got him from a sperm bank", as he had told his friend when they first shared confidences, did not make Mrs Anderson any less awesome.

Moreover, for all Ryan's complaints – that his mother's attention was the sort of brilliant light best suited to torturing people in war films, and that she was just "too much" – it was Jamie's Mum who was the problem.

"Tell me the facts again." Ryan had rigged up his bedroom as Operation Headquarters. An old basketball poster (one of his Mom's doomed attempts to keep him in touch with his American roots) had been blu-tacked, face to the wall, for use as a memo-board, and Ryan was poised in front of it with a marker.

"She's phoning horoscopes for hours every week and it's costing hundreds of pounds."

Ryan wrote 'horoscopes', 'phone', and '£££', randomly

in capital letters on the poster. "Start at the beginning," he prompted.

Jamie thought. "I suppose she used to check her horoscope in the paper, watch those people on daytime telly – you know, reading the stars and so on. When she wasn't working, and Dad wasn't around–"

Ryan wrote 'TV', and 'paper', beside 'PHONE', and drew a circle round them, then found another space for 'DAD'.

Jamie had been lying on the carpet, but sat up when she saw his addition.

"Cross that out," she said. "That's got nothing to do with it. If he's there, she can't watch stuff like that on telly because he has his programmes on, that's all. It's not like she's waiting to get rid of him so she can do stuff, more like–" Ryan raised an eyebrow "–more like, she does different stuff when he's not there," she tailed off.

"We put it all up, then we decide what's relevant," Ryan decreed, "not before."

"But you make it look like she's having an affair or something."

"Is she?" Ryan asked, with interest.

"No!"

"How do you know?"

"I just do."

Ryan turned towards his poster, marker hovering and

Jamie said, "Don't you dare."

He sighed and left it, or at least wrote nothing. "So, your Dad knows your Mum spends hours – and loads of money – on fortune tellers."

"No," Jamie admitted. "I'm sure he doesn't know, because I'd have heard the roof flying off the house if he found out. He'd go nuclear."

"So how come he doesn't know?" Ryan didn't let Jamie to answer. "Either he's really thick, and notices nothing, or she's being clever at hiding things." Ryan suddenly registered Jamie's reaction. "Sorry, Jamie, I'm just being objective, I don't mean–"

"That my Dad's a moron and my Mum's a liar?"

"That's not what I said."

"You might as well have. I don't know why I bothered telling you." Jamie pulled herself up and headed for the door, shaking off Ryan's attempt to hold her back.

"Wait. I've got an idea. Look at this."

Jamie hesitated, her cheeks still flaming with angry colour, while Ryan turned back to the poster and drew an arrow from 'paper' to 'telly' to 'phone'.

"It's getting worse, isn't it?" he stabbed the poster. "She's checking it more often, and she wants direct contact with the fortune teller now – and it's costing more, isn't it? The phone bills are getting more expensive. Am I right?"

Jamie slowly closed the door handle, nodding reluctantly. "Yes. It's getting to be every day sometimes, if she thinks no one will notice. And I know we haven't got the money, Ry, so I don't know how she's paying."

"So, she's hiding things – not by lying," he added hastily, "just by doing things so as other people won't know."

Jamie shrugged. "She does all the money stuff so Dad wouldn't know about that. And I sometimes hear bits of the phone calls, but with her and Dad on shifts, they're never home together, or Dad's down the pub, so he wouldn't hear, and Gareth's always out or in the coal shed, practising with the band."

"So, what have you heard on the phone."

"Not a lot. It's mostly her listening for ages, then she asks a question like, "What should I do about this problem in work?" and she'll say what the problem is – it's always really boring, like a security guard trying to get extra discount or something like that.

Or she'll say she's thinking of making some changes round the house, is this a good time? I thought she was talking to a friend at first, but then I heard her saying, "Thank you, Madam Sosotris," or some name like that, and then I kept hearing odd words like 'Capricorn', and I suddenly knew what was going on.

And I knew people would just laugh about it if I said

anything, because it's just normal, isn't it, reading your horoscopes and that."

"Not if you start believing in them."

"So why do you read them?"

"I don't. But you *have* been known to read them aloud to me."

There was a silence. "Do you think there's anything in it, Ry?"

"No way." Less certainly, "No, no way."

"But there's loads of people check on their stars before they do things, even world leaders."

"Like who?"

"I don't know off the top my head, do I!"

Ryan grinned. "So, we find out. Step 1, know your enemy. And Mr Travis is looking for stuff for the school newsletter, so we write it up and publish it."

"Oh no," Jamie groaned. "Mr Travis is *always* looking for stuff for the school newsletter."

"So, we help ourselves *and* we help him. We prove that horoscopes are rubbish, that fortune tellers are con-artists, and we help your Mum. And I didn't laugh at you," he pointed out.

He turned again to his poster and stabbed at the progression from 'paper' to 'phone'. "And it's going to get worse again. What do you think will be the next step up after all these phone calls?"

Alone again later, Jamie reminded herself, "Horoscopes are rubbish and fortune tellers are con-artists." She looked at the search on her computer screen and started work, ignoring the nagging voice in her head, "And what if they're not?"

CHAPTER 2

WRITTEN IN THE STARS

I bet you're Scorpio, aren't you? Yes? Then I'm clairvoyant.

No? Then I bet you know what your star sign is, and the names of the others.

But I bet you don't know why some people think that the movements of these twelve constellations say something about you and your life.

4,000 years ago, star-gazers in Iraq saw that the sun seemed to take a set path, like a belt, among the stars. These early astronomers divided this path into twelve sections, and called each section after a constellation they could see there.

They made maps of the skies, which are the basis of the modern science of astronomy and it was the ancient Greeks who called the sun path by the name "Zodiac", which meant "belt".

In the past, astronomers were also astrologers; they believed that the pattern of star movement decided the personalities and fates of human beings.

WHAT IS A STAR SIGN?

Your star sign is the section of the Zodiac where you would see the sun on the day you were born. The Zodiac constellations 4,000 years ago (also called the Star Signs or the Sun Signs) were:

Aries, Taurus, Gemini, Cancer, Leo, Virgo, Libra, Scorpio, Sagittarius, Capricorn, Aquarius and Pisces

WHAT IS A HOROSCOPE?

It is a map of the sky made by astrologers to show a particular moment such as someone's birth.

The horoscopes in magazines are general summaries based on these maps and astrologers often say that they are not good because they are not for an individual.

WHAT DO ASTROLOGERS DO?

They interpret their maps of the skies. From horoscopes, they describe someone's personality and predict events, advising people on good times and bad times to carry out certain actions, according to where the planets and the star signs will be. The horoscopes are sometimes very complicated star maps, but this does not make it any more scientific to link them to human behaviour.

If the sun is gradually covered over by a black circle, in the middle of the day, so that everything goes dark, do you run around screaming that the world is ending?

In the past, when people didn't know about eclipses, this is what they thought.

Astrology maps are just as out of date. We now know it is not the sun that travels and that star movements change. We know there are more than five planets and we know that there are thirteen Zodiac signs.

5 PLANETS IN OUR SOLAR SYSTEM?

Astrologers only include Mercury, Venus, Mars, Jupiter and Saturn in their charts because these are the only ones the early star-gazers knew about. We now know of Neptune and Uranus, and about dwarf planets. Pluto was first called a planet, then a dwarf planet, and there are still arguments about definitions.

13 ZODIAC SIGNS?

The constellation Ophiuchus (pictured as the Serpent-Carrier) has moved into the sun path in the last 4,000 years so some Sagittarians are really Ophiuchans. Also, because of star movement, Pisceans are really Arians.

Astronomy is sky science; astrology is sky magic

As Jamie added some of her own research into the article Ryan had emailed her, she heard her mother calling, "Goodnight love", as she left for her night shift at Tesco. Dad would be home in half an hour so this was a good time for a fridge raid, and Jamie followed the rumblings of her stomach into the kitchen. *The Evening Post* was open on the table and Jamie wondered afterwards what it was that drew her attention to the small ad.

PSYCHIC EXTRAVAGANZA!
Make the most of your life with the help of
fully qualified
astrologers,
clairvoyants
and mediums

FREE readings in stars, crystals, cards and palms
at *the Golden Sheep Hotel*

26th, 27th and 28th March
10am – 5pm

The one certainty in life was that her mother had noticed the ad too. What had Ryan said about things getting worse?

A patch of daffodils risked a show of brightest yellow on a green bank that was steep enough to make it difficult for passing kids to kick the heads off the flowers. As the Year 7 pupils charged down the bank onto the field, pushing each other into the puddles, and then dashing off on some other mad game, Ryan sat on the wall at the top, consulting some sheets of paper. Jamie, sitting beside him, flicked her curly black hair out of her eyes, picked up a sheet of paper caught by the breeze, and passed it back to Ryan, along with a teaspoon, which he used as a paperweight.

Neither of them bothered to consider *why* a teaspoon was lying in the school grounds. If you wasted time reflecting on the varied litter in the daily school landscape, you would never get around to real thinking. And Ryan was in deep thought, observed closely by three classmates.

"Kelly first," Ryan finally announced.

"Do you have to hold my hand or what?" asked Kelly.

Jamie cut in quickly, "That's palm reading, not horoscopes. You've already told Ryan your birthday, so that's all he needs to do your horoscope."

"All right then, let's hear it?" Kelly grinned at her friends.

"19th December, so you're Sagittarius, which means that you're outgoing, adventurous and fun-loving." Kelly nodded at every pronouncement. "You like travel, and meeting new people, and you're very creative, talented, probably at music." Kelly stopped nodding and glared at him.

"But you know I sing, so what's the point of pretending you can tell all that from the stars? And I bet she," Kelly jerked an accusing finger at Jamie, "told you the other stuff. She could have got Gareth to talk about me."

"I told you they were just out to take the piss," said Donna, turning to go. "I don't know why we came."

Kelly rounded on her. "Because this is Gareth's sister, because these two know stuff, and because I want to find out something." She challenged Ryan, "Go on then, tell me something I don't know."

"Well, I've only told you the good things about Sagittarians and your faults are that you go over the top and you tend to argue."

"That's crap. People say that, but they always start it, and I don't see any harm in saying what you think! I suppose you do, do you? Think that, just because I'm a girl, I should keep quiet and look cute or something?"

"Er no, not that you don't," Ryan added hastily, "look all right that is, but anyway," he hurried on, feeling a sudden chill from the wall beside him. "This is the best bit. From looking at these charts, I help you with making the best of the week ahead, so you know when to look out for trouble and when it's going to be a good day."

"Let me see those charts."

Kelly moved the teaspoon, and looked at the diagrams: circles with interior circles and segments, numbers and symbols, and words like 'longitude', 'conjunction', 'ascendant' and 'mutable'. She deliberately made her eyes cross, a talent that amused her friends in many a dull lesson.

"Worse than Geography," was the verdict. She threw the papers back at Ryan. "Do you really understand all this?"

Ryan gave her his most honest look. "Yes."

"And it tells you what's going to happen?"

"Yes."

"OK then. Go on."

Ryan shut his eyes and reflected, then consulted his sheets again. "There will be a crisis for you on Wednesday, when Neptune is in Scorpio. This is not good for you so when you are asked to make a big decision, you should stall, play for time, or it will turn out badly.

You should give your answer on Friday, when Venus is in the third house – that is definitely going to work out as you would like it to, especially if you talk to your friends before you make your mind up."

WHAT IS YOUR STAR SIGN?

ELEMENT	SIGN	BIRTH DATES
Fire	Aries	21st March–19th April
Earth	Taurus	20th April–20th May
Air	Gemini	21st May–21st June
Water	Cancer	22nd June–22nd July
Fire	Leo	23rd July–22nd August
Earth	Virgo	23rd August–22nd September
Air	Libra	23rd September–23rd October
Water	Scorpio	24th October–21st November
Fire	Sagittarius	22nd November–21st December
Earth	Capricorn	22nd December–19th January
Air	Aquarius	20th January–18th February
Water	Pisces	19th February–20th March

Kelly's face glowed. "Thanks Ryan, that's great, really useful." She hesitated. "Can you tell me–" she lowered her voice and the last words came out in a rush, "–is it going to work out for me and Gareth?"

"That's tricky," Ryan shook his head, "but not impossible. When's Gareth's birthday?"

"15th August," said Jamie and Kelly together.

Ryan checked his chart. "Leo," he pronounced.

"Is that bad?" Kelly asked anxiously.

"Two fire signs," Ryan mused. "Give me a minute." He went through the eye-shutting routine again, and consulted a different sheet of paper with the same sort of indecipherable squiggles on it. A small boy balancing nearby on the wall, apparently waiting for his turn to be pushed down the bank, stared at Ryan and yelled, "Wooooo, voodoooo, dead chickens, yeah, I'm scared", before his friend caught up with him and he vanished from sight. Ryan sighed.

"Grow up!" yelled Kelly at the invisible Year 7.

"Too many video nasties," was Jamie's view.

"Nah, I blame multi-faith Religious Education," said Ryan, before concentrating again on the job in hand. "No, not good. There is lots of passion between you…"

"You can say that again," was Donna's comment, and Marie, whose only contribution to date had been to nod her head, said, "Lots", and nodded her head.

"Shut up, you two, this is serious. And? But?" Kelly prompted.

"And you can work together well. The sparks flying are good on stage."

"That's when they sing together," Marie explained to Donna, as if she didn't know, "with the band."

"But you both like lots of attention and you both get jealous and…" Ryan suddenly seemed tired, "and the bell's going to go soon."

"Finish it," Kelly ordered.

"And there's going to be more and more arguments until you've had enough, or he's had enough." Ryan looked apologetic. "I'm sorry. But the stars only say what might happen. You can still choose."

Kelly's colour was high, her eyes too bright. "Yeah, right. Well, it's not like it's your fault anyway. Let's go."

"What about us?" asked Donna.

"Tomorrow, if you still want," Ryan told them. "And look out for the next edition of *The Afan Times* – it's got loads in it. It'll even tell you about your Chinese horoscope and how to work out who's best for you to go out with."

"See you then." The girls turned to go.

"No wait! I need to tell Kelly something" Jamie shouted over the buzzer, and her voice echoed oddly in the silence that followed.

She stumbled on, "Ryan said 'fire', and it's something about fire, I don't know, you've got to be careful about fire."

"Like don't play with it," said Kelly sarcastically. "This week or this lifetime?"

"I don't know," was Jamie's helpless reply.

"Thanks all the same, but I should keep to being the magician's assistant if I was you. At least he knows what he's on about. Even if," she shot Ryan a black look, "it's not what I want to hear."

"I thought that went very well," Ryan told Jamie after the others were out of earshot.

She turned on him. "Any particular reason for trying to split her and Gareth up?"

"But that's the point of the experiment – we show that this horoscope stuff is garbage, that people react to what they hear, and then do what they want. You don't think someone as stubborn as Kelly will split up with her boyfriend over some daft horoscope, do you? It'll just make her more determined to stay with him, and we'll have another bit of proof that horoscopes are rubbish."

"But that wasn't a real horoscope, so it doesn't work. And you're just encouraging them, telling them to look in *The Afan Times* for their Chinese horoscopes, when I thought we were trying to show it's all rubbish."

"Got to get them to read it in the first place though, haven't we. And there's no such thing as a real horoscope – they're all made up from stuff that was written down centuries ago and then some con-artist like me makes up the rest from what they can work out about the person.

Two people in a couple are always going to have arguments, and they wouldn't be together in the first place if they didn't fancy each other, so all you have to do is mix the good and the bad for a compatibility reading."

"Easy enough with Kelly," Jamie observed, "when we know so much about her. Bet you can't do it with Marie."

"You just watch. All I have to do is mix in a few bits of astrology, come out with some general comments, and they'll interpret them as they want. I mean, it's always going to be a good idea to wait before you make a decision, and talk to your friends first, and that's all I've told Kelly to do with that stuff about Wednesday and Friday."

"Hmm," was Jamie's only comment.

"That's where you made your mistake," Ryan pressed the point. "That stuff about a fire was too obvious after me talking about fire signs, too specific about what, and too vague about when, so she's not going to believe you, is she. Why did you do that anyway? I thought we'd agreed that I was going to do the reading?"

"I don't know." Jamie knew why only too well, but there was no way she was going to tell her friend what had just happened, not when they were handing in material for a newspaper article on what a load of rubbish all this fortune-telling was, not when she needed to prove what rubbish it was, for her mother's sake.

What she said was, "Let's take this stuff to Mr Travis after school and see what he thinks. We need it to be in print for my Mum to see before that thing in March."

Some things never changed. Mr Travis had a pile of exercise books in front of him, and hardly glanced at Ryan and Jamie as he held out his hand for the USB drive they gave him.

"Do it at home," he muttered, "Not worth the hassle trying to convince Cerberus that a virus check actually checks for viruses so that you can use the system. Virus checks are like librarians used to be when I was a kid, only happy when the books were all tidy on the shelves and the library silent and empty.

They're all computer experts nowadays, patrolling their firewall. That's what it is," he waggled his red pen in the air, "they think they're firemen – sorry Jamie, fire fighters – and they've kept their darling data safe. Only there's no data any more because they don't have time to 'input' as they say, and mere mortals like you are firebugs." Jamie and Ryan listened politely until there was a pause.

"Sir?" Ryan prompted. "The file's called *Horoscopes*. We're investigating astrology, applying scientific views."

"The scope of horror," Mr Travis mused, his pen continuing its red trail on an exercise book, *Next time, make paragraphs and add more detail.* "Very good, very good."

"Thank you, Sir." Ryan assumed the praise was sent in their direction, judging by the negative comments written on the book, but it was always difficult to tell.

It was easier to work out that they had been dismissed when Mr Travis nodded curtly, saying, "Jamie, Myrddin".

Ryan was using 'Myrddin', the Welsh version of Merlin, as a pen name, having adopted it two years earlier for an Eisteddfod competition piece. At first it had been a way of hiding his identity, not least from his mother, but events had made sure everyone in school knew who Myrddin was, and he kept the name because he felt it suited him. He joked with Jamie that it was one advantage of not knowing who his father was, that he could pick and choose his ancestors.

The classroom door banged behind Jamie but Mr Travis didn't even raise his head.

Jamie asked, "Do you think he'll read it before he puts it in *The Afan Times*?"

"Doubt it."

Some things never changed, but others did.

"Did you see his hair?" asked Ryan.

"Amazing. What colour was it before?"

"Brown, with lots of gray. And definitely no gel." There was no doubt that Mr Travis now sported a firmly gelled short vertical crop of black hair.

"Do you think we'll go weird when we get old?" Jamie wondered.

"You might." Ryan was still protecting his sides from some serious punches when they left the school building and he could run ahead, turning to mock her before accepting her gesture of truce, along with one last punch when she caught up with him.

Their steps settled to the comfortable pace of habit, and they didn't notice the roar of the M4 motorway as they passed under it towards the streets nestled against the hill boundary between Port Talbot and the wilds of the Afan Valley.

CHINESE HOROSCOPES

WHICH IS THE CREATURE THAT HIDES IN YOUR HEART?
A rat, ox, tiger, rabbit, dragon, snake, horse, goat (or sheep), monkey, cockerel, dog or boar?

This is the old Chinese saying about the year you were born, which, according to the Chinese calendar, is named after one of these twelve creatures.

According to legend, Lord Buddha commanded all the creatures to come to him before he left the earth, and only these twelve actually came, so he rewarded them by naming a year after each one, in the order they came to him.

Find your creature and see what it says about you (and who you should go out with). Remember that the Chinese New Year starts according to the moon, like Easter, so it is on a different date each year. If your birthday is between January 1st and January 9th you are counted in the previous year of the Western calendar.

If your birthday is between January 10th and February 15th, you will need to check which year you are in.

RAT	1948	1960	1972	1984	1996	2008	2020
OX	1949	1961	1973	1985	1997	2009	2021
TIGER	1950	1962	1974	1986	1998	2010	2022
RABBIT	1951	1963	1975	1987	1999	2011	2023
DRAGON	1952	1964	1976	1988	2000	2012	2024
SNAKE	1953	1965	1977	1989	2001	2013	2025
HORSE	1954	1966	1978	1990	2002	2014	2026
GOAT	1955	1967	1979	1991	2003	2015	2027
MONKEY	1956	1968	1980	1992	2004	2016	2028
COCKEREL	1957	1969	1981	1993	2005	2017	2029
DOG	1958	1970	1982	1994	2006	2018	2030
BOAR	1959	1971	1983	1995	2007	2019	2031

RAT: generous and easy-going but edgy when upset. Rats have good memories, love money and hate laziness. BEST WITH OX, DRAGON OR MONKEY

OX: calm, patient and hard-working. stubborn and tends to bear grudges. Likes to work through things step by step. BEST WITH RAT, RABBIT OR COCKEREL

TIGER: loving, sincere and go-getting, likes attention and hates being ignored. Jumps into decisions quickly and sometimes rashly. BEST WITH DRAGON, HORSE OR DOG

RABBIT: strong-willed but likes to be in the background, kind, hates disagreement and likes a peaceful life. BEST WITH OX, SNAKE OR GOAT

DRAGON: strong, full of energy, so original that a dragon can be seen as weird, tends to be arrogant, a leader. BEST WITH RAT, TIGER, SNAKE OR MONKEY

SNAKE: intellectual, very private and independent, suspicious, tends to think first and speak later, leads a dangerous and complex life. BEST WITH RABBIT, DRAGON OR COCKEREL

HORSE: unpredictable, falls easily in and out of love, gets its way through charm, loves exercise and finds it difficult to relax. BEST WITH TIGER, GOAT OR DOG

GOAT OR SHEEP: born worrier, easily swayed by emotions, shy, good at looking after others, very understanding and hates being criticised. BEST WITH RABBIT, HORSE OR PIG

MONKEY: inventive, problem-solver, curious, and lively company but monkeys believe their own lies and tell them often. BEST WITH RAT OR DRAGON

COCKEREL: very confident on the surface, good with money, like attention, but cockerels are less creative or competent than they appear. BEST WITH OX OR SNAKE

DOG: very honest, loyal, hardworking, always helps someone in need but can be aggressive or gloomy for no reason. BEST WITH TIGER, HORSE OR PIG

BOAR: brave, strong, makes a good teacher, unselfish and can get taken for granted, easily tricked and hot-tempered. BEST WITH RABBIT, GOAT OR DOG

A section of your class is one creature, and the rest is another, so there are only two different types of people in your whole class.

Are you really the same as all those other kids?

Or even like them in personality?

SO MAYBE THE SUN SIGNS MAKE A BETTER SYSTEM FOR SAYING WHO YOU ARE?

No! The two systems are the same in splitting all humans into twelve categories; it's just easier to see how daft this when you're in a year group in a school.

Adults who mix in different ages would be mixing with all eleven other creatures, so whether they're a 'Rabbit' or a 'Sagittarius' it comes to the same thing:

1) generalising about personality types

2) basing this on when a person was born.

Your Afan Times reporters, Jamie and Myrddin, aim to prove how stupid horoscopes really are, by some simple experiments.

Help us please!

EXPERIMENT 1

All you Geminis, and only you Geminis, come to the back of the School Hall at 1.00pm on Wednesday 18th arch for a Gemini Group Photo.

Anyone who feels like it, come to the back of the School Hall at 1.00pm on Thursday 19th March, for a Control Group Photo.

(there will be a limit on numbers)

CHAPTER 3

Jamie couldn't sleep. She was trying to remember exactly what Ryan said to Kelly before the weird feeling had happened. Something about Kelly and Gareth both being star signs, then some silly comment about sparks flying, and then everything had faded, as if Jamie was lost in a mist with voices echoing somewhere but no words that made sense.

It was as if she came to, focused again, and the first person she saw was Kelly turning to go. Then, there was an overwhelming feeling of panic, the need to rush over to Kelly, and something in her brain was screaming, "Fire, fire – get her out of the way!"

Thank God, she'd only said something, not run around, shoving Kelly out of some imaginary danger. She'd have looked a right fool, and Kelly's comments were sharp enough without giving her ammunition.

As it was, Kelly was thinking of her as Ryan's sidekick, a bumbling no-talent. Kelly might be mouthy, but when she turned that same voice to singing, it could melt the Brecons or make geriatrics dance, whichever she wanted.

So what, that Jamie got better marks in school? They weren't as good as Ryan's, and there was nothing she could say was her talent. She was ordinary, that was the truth of it, and she shouldn't be surprised if Ryan wanted a more interesting friend. But not, her brain went around in contradictory circles, a friend who was interesting because she had premonitions.

One premonition, she corrected herself. And it was just a mad moment, like Ryan said, a subconscious suggestion from what he was saying. *And it's not as if anything's going to happen to Kelly, so just forget you opened your stupid mouth, Jamie Williams, and concentrate on what's important.*

She punched the pillow, rolled over to another uncomfortable position in bed and wondered what her mother would make of the article in *The Afan Times*. Jamie had made a point of giving it to her mother personally, saying, "There's one of our articles in here that I'd really like to talk to you about," and she'd wanted to giggle because it was just like when her mother had given her a booklet on 'girls growing up', only with the roles reversed.

She hoped she could make a better job of the discussion than her mother had of explaining 'growing up'. It was clear that her mother didn't have a clue about sex, and that it would be much more educational, and less embarrassing for both of them, if Jamie stuck to her usual sources of knowledge to answer life's interesting questions.

Mrs Williams had been on her way to work at Tesco, but had promised to read it before Jamie came home from school the next day. So, what was Jamie going to say to her? Obviously, her mother was going to be gutted at realising how gullible she'd been. She'd be upset that she'd wasted so much time and money on total garbage, and she might be angry at the people who'd conned her.

Jamie would reassure her, she'd say, "It's not your fault, there's loads of people get taken in by this stuff", because it always made you feel better if you thought you weren't the only one. Jamie remembered going over a Maths exam paper with a really sarcastic teacher, and, on every question, he asked who'd got it wrong. It wasn't too bad when your hand went up with loads of others, but the poor sod whose solitary hand went up for Question 12 had a personal lecture in front of the whiteboard.

Yes, Jamie thought, *make her feel she's not the only one, and then be really positive about saving all that money. Make her think about it as saving, not look back on what's gone already.*

And if her Mum did get angry at being conned, perhaps that was a good thing. When Jamie got angry, she did something about it. This wasn't the first time she'd campaigned in the school newspaper and she was willing to speak up for what she believed in, so she could help her Mum. Perhaps they'd even write to *The Evening Post* about it all. She thought of her Dad. Maybe not. Or maybe with a pen name.

Jamie was pleased with herself. Maybe she did have a talent

after all, a talent for helping people. And campaigning in newspapers. It wasn't just Ryan's ideas, or his writing, and he'd said they were a team, so maybe he didn't think she was so boring. Maybe she was just having a lack-self-esteem-moment like they were all supposed not to do, especially in their GCSE years, according to yesterday's assembly.

The pillow was starting to feel softer, having assumed the shape of a tortured sheep, but Jamie bashed it once more for good measure, and decided that no one would know if she cheated. She reached over to open the bottom drawer in the small unit beside her bed, and hauled out something gray and furry, pinching one rounded ear between her fingers.

A bit of stuffing was falling out the arm of her childhood teddy bear, where it had worn thin from years of lying under her head. It was only six months since Gareth's teasing had led to Bertie's exile in the drawer, and this was a special occasion. She tucked Bertie into his customary place and drifted into contented sleep.

It was only one lesson she was mitching, Kelly told herself, as she headed down the road to the college, and it wasn't as if it was a real subject anyway. Careers! The only career advice she needed was how to get a recording contract, and, somehow, she didn't think the Geography teacher who dished out computer forms once a fortnight in the Careers lesson would be of any use. There wasn't even a tick-box for what she wanted, and when she'd tried saying so, she'd been treated much the same as the boy who wanted to be a bodyguard. If he only knew what Kelly was like outside school, he'd treat her with a bit more respect, that teacher – and all the others.

She'd worked herself silly over the last year, most days after school in Gareth's coal shed with the band, picking up a bit of guitar from Chris, the bassist. If only she could have a guitar of her own – but there was no chance of that. When she couldn't meet up with the boys, she'd just have to practise as she always had, to the music in her head.

What a year it had been! When she remembered the moment Gareth said to her, "Do you want to sing with us?" she still felt like she was floating. All those times she'd sat, listening, longing to join in, and then gone home to sing her heart out with an imaginary mike in front of the mirror; they'd all been worth it.

And then that date ringed in kisses in her diary, when Gareth said it would be good for them to practise a duet, without the others, just the two of them. She knew, as soon as he said the song title, that it was going to happen, that he'd written the song specially for her, and, when he kissed her, she felt shy and awkward and beautiful all at the same time.

It worked between them, and the band went down a storm at the school disco, with Kelly up front. They'd had some offers of gigs since then, but Kelly had to be evasive about her age. She bet Charlotte bloody Church hadn't had these problems when she was fifteen.

Still, if there was one thing Kelly was good at, as well as singing, then it was passing for eighteen. So, she shouldn't have any problem mixing with the college students this afternoon, especially as she'd be with Gareth.

It was one of those fresh March days that tricks you into thinking spring has arrived, and it looked as if the college fun-day was going to hit lucky, weather-wise. The day was in aid of *Sport for Life*, and run by Gareth's department, Sports Science.

"Yes, but what's it for," Kelly had asked him.

"Sport," was the answer.

"Well that's really useful," Kelly had told him but her sarcasm was wasted. She'd never mentioned to her Sports Science boyfriend that she was one of those who always managed to forget her games kit, or have a conveniently timed period and a forged note.

As Gareth had seen her dancing and singing for two hours, electric with energy, he assumed that she was the life and soul of every school team, and she hadn't bothered to disillusion him. It was clear to Kelly that Jamie must have let comments pass without contradicting them, and she was grateful for that. Another one not keen on Games, Jamie, but she didn't seem as clumsy these days.

God, Kelly thought, *we're all growing up*. Which was all very well in some ways, but it didn't look to her like too much fun. And fun was what she was here for.

What had Gareth said? "You gotta come, girl. There's a bouncy castle".

Not the world's best with words, her Gareth, unless he could think a bit and write them to music of course, but to a loving girlfriend who'd seen his face light up, the words 'bouncy castle' held the magnetic attraction he intended, and here she was.

And there *it* was, twenty feet high, a heaving rubber structure with cartoon towers at the corners and eighteen-year-old boys scrambling over each other like puppies in basket, squealing like them too. Kelly spotted her particular puppy, waved to him, and got a frantic, "Come on up," sign in return.

She sighed and took off her shoes. She'd read plenty of advice in magazines about saying no to boys who pushed you beyond what you wanted, but none of it had mentioned bouncy castles so she'd better show she was up for it. And then there was nothing much but bouncing, bruises and swopping smiles as you saw each other at strange angles. Jolly, canned music mingled with the strange "yo" and "woo" calls of students, mostly boys.

When Kelly felt her smile slipping along with her stomach, she yelled, "Time out for me", at a horizontally passing Gareth and lowered herself onto grass that carried on heaving under her feet. She sat, quickly.

Once the world seemed relatively stationary, she looked around, noticing for the first time the sign *Daycare* in primary colours and large joined writing, posted above some door-size windows. Pressed against the windows were the faces of the daycare inhabitants. Like little zoo animals, the children were staring wistfully at the bouncy castle. Kelly looked again at the students and back at the sad little faces. Just like she'd been, she thought, watching the band and hoping without real hope that she'd be allowed to join in. It just wasn't fair.

She sat, brooding. So, was she just going to sit there? No way. She bounced her way back to Gareth, grabbed his arm to attempt simultaneous bouncing, and yelled in his ear, getting butted in the nose once for her troubles. He gave her the thumbs up, had a last bounce, and went off to talk to the tutors.

Five minutes later, disgruntled students were being

encouraged to leave their trampolining, and a crocodile of little ones, holding hands in pairs, filed out from the daycare classroom with a nursery nurse at the head, and another one at the back. They weren't the only ones holding hands as Kelly beamed at Gareth.

She watched the antics on the bouncy castle. The children were like hedgehogs, curling up, stretching out and rolling again, their joy contagious, but Gareth grew restless.

"Let's go."

Kelly followed him round the back of the sports buildings, towards a canteen packed with students and visitors who'd come for the fun-day. Inevitably, odd cans of beer had infiltrated the grounds, and a few students were showing signs of where it had gone, friendly scuffles deteriorating in places to more serious signs of conflict.

Perhaps more than beer, Kelly thought, noting one man with vacant eyes, sitting propped against a classroom wall, waving his arms vaguely. She held Gareth's hand a little more tightly, off her own territory and wary, but he seemed relaxed as he followed some invisible path.

Perhaps it was that alertness that saved her, made her react quickly when she heard shouting behind her, someone calling drunkenly, as if joking, "Ready, aim…" and it was Jamie's voice she heard yelling, "fire!" at exactly the moment she dived to the ground, jarring her shoulder and twisting a hand as she landed on it.

Gareth was calling someone every swearword he knew and running. Kelly raised herself up and turned to work out what was going on, in time to see Gareth and someone else both being restrained by some students. Kelly winced, got up and walked over as a tutor arrived, switching off the cell-phone she'd just used.

Two more tutors arrived and everyone was talking over each other, so it was a miracle that Gareth's voice was heard at all, but Kelly was used to listening for that voice, and for her it was the only one speaking. His tones were high and shaky.

"This—" he glanced at the tutors and dropped the adjective, "—moron used *that* on my girlfriend."

That was now in a tutor's hands and Kelly recognised it as an air gun.

The blanking-moron seemed a little more sober now and a bit aggrieved.

"S'only an air gun and I wasn't shooting at her. Was shooting at Paul, and he were asking for it. Wasn't going to hit him neither, just frighten him a bit, like."

"Did anyone else see what happened?" a tutor asked.

"Yeah," a girl with a pierced eyebrow admitted reluctantly. "He was pointing that thing all over the place, talking big, then he said he'd 'show Paul' and pointed towards him," she indicated, "but that girl walked in front of Paul when the boy shot, so he could have shot her instead if she hadn't dived down."

"Except he couldn't hit the ground with his own piss, the state on him," someone else commented. "Er, sorry and all that, but it's true."

"Are you all right?" Kelly was startled to find someone talking to her. She blushed.

"Yeah, fine." She shrugged it off.

"What a prat. Come on, Gareth, he's not worth it."

A tutor insisted on taking some details from them, but once it was clear that neither Kelly nor Gareth had seen anything because they'd been walking away, they were allowed to go.

"If you don't sort him out, I will," Gareth told the tutors, who achieved tactical deafness and let him go.

It was only later, in the coal shed, that Kelly started shaking and, when Gareth took her in his arms and cuddled her, she began to sob, sniffing from time to time and muttering, "Right pisser".

"I don't understand." Jamie's smile was fading, while her mother's hadn't wavered. "Haven't you read our article?"

"Of course I read it, Jamie, and it's very nice, very well written."

"Nice," Jamie repeated, disbelieving. "But it's what we're saying that counts, it's important. People," and here she gave her mother a significant look, "should know that horoscopes are rubbish, and paying for them's a rip-off."

"Of course." Her Mum's smile didn't falter. "You and Ryan said it really well. They're too general for anyone with any sense to believe them – they're just a bit of fun. They only use the position of the sun, and you need a personal chart showing all the factors to get a real reading.

People actually express their moon sign far more than their sun sign, and I find the position of Jupiter very important for me at the moment. It's the planet that governs how we grow and how we add to our understanding of the world."

"But–" Jamie was cut off by her mother.

"But people realise all that, when they try the real thing, a personal horoscope by someone with proper qualifications – there's just no comparison.

And there are cowboys in all kinds of jobs – builders, electricians – you only have to watch those television programmes to see what some of them get up to, so of course you have to pick and choose people who know what they're doing, professionals."

Which was the point where Jamie lost her temper. "So, they're professionals are they? Those witches that you spend hours phoning? That you're spending hundreds of pounds on? You think that's what Dad would say?"

Her mother coloured up but was still calm when she spoke. "Your Dad might not understand, Jamie, but I think you could if you tried. You're almost a woman now, and, if I know you, I think you have opinions of your own, and don't just agree with everything someone else thinks, even if someone is a good friend."

She pushed her point home. "Even if *someone* is male."

It was Jamie's turn to flush. Was she too easily swayed by Ryan's views? *The best form of defence...*

"And the money?"

"Perhaps you'd ask in future if you'd like to look at my bills and accounts." Her mother's tone would freeze rivers.

Jamie remembered how clever she'd felt rifling through her mother's neat files, and her colour deepened as her Mum carried on, "But seeing as you ask, it will pay for itself before the end of the year. It's just like going on a college course – you pay to learn how to make the most of yourself, to improve your life."

"Doesn't look to me like there's anything wrong with your life!" was Jamie's feeble attempt at a parting shot. It backfired.

"There's a lot you don't know, Jamie," was the sad reply, accompanied by a weary smile that twisted Jamie's heart into a million aching pieces.

"I don't understand," she heard her own voice whining. Her Mum seemed to be following some internal debate, and then to reach some kind of conclusion.

"We are all linked, but some of us more closely than others, and it might be good for both of us if you have a reading yourself." Jamie was speechless. "Not one of these mickey mouse things in the papers, a real one with a proper clairvoyant. My day off is Thursday next week, and I'm going to a fortune-telling event. You're on school holidays – you can come with me if you want. Think about it. Now, what am I doing for tea?" Jamie's mother opened the fridge door and sighed at what the shelves offered, while Jamie took off to her room, wondering where she had gone wrong, and what on earth she was going to do about it.

CHAPTER 4

Ryan looked at the scrap of black humanity staring at him with huge, pleading eyes. "Why me?" he asked. "Why should I have anything in common with Sam?"

"I'd have thought was obvious," replied Mrs Delango, the Head of Year, who had summoned Ryan to a lunchtime meeting in her office.

"Well, it isn't."

Mrs Delango sighed. "You've coped so well with being the only black pupil in our school, Ryan, we thought you'd be a wonderful role model for Sam?"

We? Who's we? "Well, now he's here, there's two of us, so he shouldn't have a problem." Ryan looked with deep disdain at the Year 7 pupil whose uniform looked as it had come straight off an ironing board.

Ryan couldn't meet the pleading look in the liquid brown eyes that seemed to fill a face still chubby with childhood, and he inspected the boy's feet. He was wearing shoes. What was the matter with the boy? Didn't he have trainers?

"Sam's mother thinks it's very important he has a role model." Ah. So they did have something in common, after all. Perhaps that explained the shoes. Ryan remembered all those artificial attempts at male bonding by the various men his mother had talked into playing role model for him, to keep him 'balanced'. With her as a mother? Was she serious?

"All right," he said grudgingly, ignoring the way Sam bounced in his seat. "What's involved in this mentoring then?"

Jamie was sitting in their usual fine-weather place on the wall, expecting peace and quiet, with Ryan otherwise occupied on some mysterious business with the Head of Year. She was surprised to see Kelly approaching, alone, and with none of the swagger that she affected when with her gang. This was out-of-school Kelly, the one Jamie could get on with, the one she could understand her brother having a thing for. If only *this* Kelly was allowed to show more often, Jamie thought, waiting for the other girl to speak first.

"I haven't told Gareth," Kelly said quietly, "all that's happened, cos it's a bit too weird." For the second time with Kelly, Jamie had a premonition. She knew what Kelly was going to say next and that she wasn't going to like it.

Jamie was still mulling over whether or not to tell Ryan about

Kelly's near-accident, and add another complication to their discussion as to whether Jamie should go along with her Mum to the fortune-telling, when Ryan himself loped into view. No one else moved the way he did, as if he weighed nothing and could float above the ground if he chose to, or lightly touch down as he flowed along, just to fit in with what normal people did. He was talking before he reached her, so she decided she'd leave her news for another time.

"… right little runt, he is too. As if it's not bad enough that he's about as cool as the Tory leader, he's thick as two short planks as well. And I'm supposed to do paired reading with him."

"Why on earth did you say you'd do it?"

"God knows." Ryan was gloomy. "I can't even say he reminded me of me. I've got more chance improving his reading than getting him streetwise. Oh no, don't look, don't look – too late."

He grinned warmly at the small boy, hovering near enough to intrude, but not so near he was within clouting distance. Ryan dismissed the thought; clouting had not been included in mentor's duties. A pity, but there it was.

"Sam, this is Jamie. You and I need to talk, about when we're going to see each other," Sam beamed, "and when we're not going to see each other." Sam nodded like a model dog in a car back-window, to show he really really understood.

"See what you mean," said Jamie. "Cute though. Perhaps I'll get one."

"All the black ones have gone," Ryan teased her, as Sam moved to the furthest edge of their vision and continued to watch them with open admiration.

CHAPTER 5

The end of term zoomed towards them, schoolwork occasionally interrupting their quest for reportage. They were pleased with the photographs. Having borrowed the English Department's digital camera, they organised the gaggle of volunteers who turned up on two gloomy lunchtimes.

Predictably, there were many more younger ones, but Jamie pointed out that it didn't matter as long as that was true on both days, which it was bound to be. They got rid of six gate-crashers who slunk off after Ryan's speech on the importance of it being Gemini today, and only Gemini.

Then they arranged their twenty-four guinea-pigs on the steps up to B-block and Jamie, the designated photographer, took a few snaps, checked them, clouted two small boys and told everyone, "Do it again and no two-finger-signs or you're out of it."

Satisfied, Jamie was ready to let the Geminis go, when a thought struck her.

"Hang on a minute." She explained to Ryan, "Tomorrow's group has got to have Gemini in to be fully representative, right? So, we want a couple of these to come back, to give us the right sort of proportion."

Ryan took the point. "OK, people, you can go, and don't

come back tomorrow, except for *you* and *you*." He held back a couple of Year 7s, cutting off their protest that they had been wiping their noses or faces, or hair out of their eyes, and that no way had they been waving two fingers in the air.

"A word," Ryan said.

Jamie was clicking buttons on the camera. It was a smart piece of machinery, and she could really get used to the feel of its strap round her shoulder, ready to aim, frame and fire. She liked the professional feel of it, imagined walking to the front of a crowd, showing her press pass, "Jamie Williams, from *The Daily Mail*."

Ryan interrupted her daydreams. "So, same again tomorrow?"

"Yes, but probably more will turn up, and we'll have to keep it to twenty-four."

"What, two of each zodiac sign?"

"Naaa, too fussy. As long as we've got a couple of Gemini, and a random mix, that'll make the point. And you know we haven't really got a big enough sample."

"We could get more," suggested Ryan, with a gleam in his eye.

Jamie shook her head. "Then you wouldn't see the faces in the photo. No, it's the picture that will make the point – people don't think their way through the numbers."

This worried Ryan. "But they should."

"They don't." Jamie was definite. "Look at my Mum. It's like a bit of her brain has gone missing over this, and it's there for everything else, so we're not going to change her mind with logic."

"So, what are we going to do?"

"Carry on with the copy for the next issue, for starters."

"How about a big headline to go with the photos: One of these photos shows only Geminis – can you tell which one?"

"It's not exactly snappy, is it. We need to work on that. And then Plan B."

"What's Plan B?"

"I don't know yet, but I think I'll have to go to this bloody fortune-telling event. Know your enemy, and all that. And I want you there too, so we can compare notes afterwards."

Ryan brightened, recovering from the impossible notion that logic might not be enough. "I could go undercover."

Jamie looked at her tall, black friend. "You're good," she told him, "but you're not that good."

'Know your enemy' seemed to be as far as they could get with Plan B, and at least offered them more material for *The Afan Times*, so they made a list of possible research topics. So far, the list read:

crystals
palm reading
salt
ouija boards
spiritualists
ghosts
water divining
metal detecting
good luck and bad luck
mind reading
tarot cards
psychological profiling
murderers
voodoo, chicken entrails
rebirth
hypnosis

They looked critically at the list.

"How the hell did salt get on the list?" asked Jamie.

"S'obvious: I looked up crystals, like crystal balls, and like on the advert for this fortune-telling event, then I was looking at types of crystals, and then I was looking at salt and how it's made. Did you know there's salt mines in North Wales?"

"What, underground, like white coal?"

"No, stupid, it's from the sea. Our readers would be really interested in how they get it."

"No, Ry, they wouldn't. And you're getting distracted. This isn't just word association you know. And what about 'ghosts'. What has that got to do with anything?"

"That is definitely relevant," Ryan defended. "Some clair-voyants say they have 'spirit guides' so to believe *that*, you have to believe in ghosts, and some of them believe in rebirth, so these spirit guides are getting reborn."

"OK," Jamie conceded, linking 'rebirth', 'spiritualists', 'ghosts' and 'Ouija board', "but it's not just any old ghost stories or we'll go off on a total tangent."

"I thought you could borrow the camera and shoot some paranormal phenomena."

Jamie was tempted. "But we know there's nothing there, so shooting nothing's a bit difficult. How do you prove there's nothing? People will just believe you missed it or whatever."

"We could set up a video camera?"

"No. Even if we could get one, I don't want to be some sort of ghost-buster. Anyway, it's all been done before and I'm really not interested."

"OK then, so what's all this about water divining and metal detecting?" Ryan countered. "I don't see what that's got to do with anything."

"I was just brainstorming and they looked really interesting – I thought we could get one of those forked twigs – or some people use a special stone on a string – and go looking for water–"

"In Wales? Do you seriously think there's anywhere we wouldn't find it?"

"Or borrow a metal detector and look for ancient coins or jewelry or something…" Jamie tailed off and sighed. "Cross them off?"

"Cross them off."

Jamie did so, saying, "And you cannot be serious with the voodoo stuff!"

"Discovering my roots, man." Jamie looked at him sceptically. "And it goes back a long way, connects up with ancient Rome. The generals used to check out the insides of a dead chicken before major battles." Ryan glanced at his friend. "No dead chickens?"

"No dead chickens." Jamie crossed out 'voodoo'. "Let's start with the stuff that's going to be in this fortune-telling event."

Ryan looked at the newspaper advert again. "How about I do palm-reading and you do cards."

"OK."

✦ PALMISTRY ✦

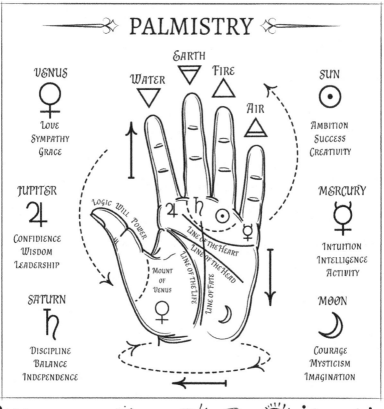

VENUS
Love
Sympathy
Grace

WATER

EARTH

FIRE

AIR

SUN
Ambition
Success
Creativity

JUPITER
Confidence
Wisdom
Leadership

Logic Will Power

Line of the Heart

Line of the Head

Mount of Venus

Line of the Life

Line of Fate

MERCURY
Intuition
Intelligence
Activity

SATURN
Discipline
Balance
Independence

MOON
Courage
Mysticism
Imagination

IF YOUR LIFE LINE is …

LONG, STRONG AND UNBROKEN, lucky you — so's your life likely to be.

FAINT, get stocked up with aspirin — you'll need lots of it.

DOUBLE, you're not necessarily schizo. You could face a major crossroads with two very different outcomes and you will have to live with knowing both possibilities.

SHORT, tough luck, sunshine. Make the most of each day and think like a winner — challenge the fates.

IS THERE A BREAK IN THE LINE?

Watch out for a major crisis, perhaps an accident, a major illness or an emotional storm but you'll come through it.

IF YOUR HEAD LINE is …

STRONG AND STRAIGHT, you know what you want and go for it. Everyone around you knows what you want too — you're a bit of a steamroller

IS FAINT AND UNCERTAIN, you can't decide whether you're indecisive or not — perhaps you are, this week.

IF YOUR FATE LINE …

STARTS AT THE WRIST, you got off the starting blocks of life right from babyhood. The later this starts, the longer you spend wondering what to do with your life.

STOPS HALF-WAY, so does the planning! Look out for an adventurous second half.

HAS ISLANDS, DOTS, FINE LINES, you could worry for Wales — chill!

OH NO! NOT THE ACE OF SWORDS! WHAT ARE TAROT CARDS?

Tarot cards are the great-great-great grandparents of a modern deck of cards. There are 78 cards divided into two groups of Arcana which means "Mysteries": 22 Major Arcana and 56 Minor Arcana.

MAJOR ARCANA are key characters or aspects of our world and represent stages in spiritual development. They are the Fool, the Magician, the High Priestess, the Empress, the Emperor, the Teacher, the Lovers, Strength, the Hermit, the Wheel of Fortune, Justice, the Hanged Man, Death, Temperance, the Devil, the Tower, the Star, the Moon, the Sun, Judgement, the World.

MINOR ARCANA are similar to a modern pack of cards but have four court cards in each suit instead of three. They are the page, the knight, the queen and the king.

The four suits are swords (spades), cups (hearts), wands (clubs) and pentacles (diamonds), representing the four elements air, water, fire and earth, in that order.

USE YOUR HIDDEN PSYCHIC TALENTS.

First, find the picture card in the Minor Arcana that represents you — try the page in the suit that matches the element of your sun sign. It's all about interpretation and the cards are just a tool, so go with the flow — if you prefer a different picture card, you're the boss. Put this card on the table.

Try a simple 3 card reading using just the Major Arcana. Shuffle and draw one card for each place.

Past X + Present X + Future X

Now read them. So, what does the Fool mean? An early stage in learning something? Innocence? Use the pictures, the ideas and your own instincts to say what these cards are telling you. Expand your spread to more cards on each row, and add in the Minor Arcana. So, what does an upside-down 10 of Pentacles mean and how does it change the meaning of the Fool beside it? There are systems giving meanings to Tarot cards; the 10 of Pentacles is associated with permanence and stability so, combined with the Fool, it could suggest being ignorant of something that is a threat to your family life.

Now wear a bright scarf round your head, call yourself Gypsy Rosalie and remember to start off with the magic words "Yes, I take a credit card." The reading might be traditional but the good old days when silver crossed the palm have changed with inflation.

CHAPTER 6

Jamie queued with her mother behind several other women, waiting to pay their entry fee in the hotel lobby. She couldn't get over how ordinary everyone looked: the women in their shopping clothes, some carrying a bag with a loaf of bread or packet of crisps poking out the top; the two women efficiently collecting money, giving tickets and saying it was fine for them to pop in and out during the day without paying again; and even the dozen or so people waiting for clients, in the large room that had been lined with stalls like at a school fete.

They were standing, chatting, or sitting behind their stalls, reading leaflets, or arranging books, cards, sparkling crystals in attractive display. They were wearing a range of T-shirts, jeans, and dresses but there was no sign of bright headscarves. The only hint of gypsy style was in a tiered skirt, an off-shoulder white blouse, a pair of hooped ear-rings, but that was just fashion.

Were these really clairvoyants, mediums, psychic loonies? Jamie's mother was already charging ahead, making for someone who was smiling in recognition, but Jamie lingered a moment on the doorsill, looking back at the queue.

Then she grinned, relieved. Ryan wasn't difficult to spot.

When had he grown quite so tall? She imagined not knowing who that was, that head and shoulders standing out, like — like Ryan… and she couldn't. There was a ripple of awkwardness around him, just a hint of extra personal space, of which he seemed blithely unaware as he concentrated on some interior dialogue. He caught her eye, gave her a thumbs-up, and motioned her to get in there, so she did.

Her mother's gesture summoned her, so Jamie went over, to be introduced to Naomi. Interesting name, Jamie thought, but not weird. Probably even her real name. All round the room, women were settling one-to-one at tables or taking a seat in the waiting area, where a notice-board advertised,

Free demonstration reading
at 11.00am, 12.00am, 2.00pm and 3pm

"You were right about Wednesday," her mother was telling Naomi, whose ear-rings jiggled about and caught the light as she nodded, highlighting the Celtic swirls cut into silver teardrop shapes. The same motif was picked out on a pendant that swung in and out of the open neckline of Naomi's white blouse.

More like a waitress, thought Jamie, *white blouse, black bootcut trousers, zipped ankle boots, hair tied back in a scrunchy.* She'd wondered about getting a waitressing job herself, to try and get some money towards university, but then she imagined holding trays with plates and drinks on them, and it was all too easy to imagine customers jumping around after being scalded by hot coffee, or wiping tomato sauce off their trousers and fishing chips out of their laps.

Her mother had saved her from testing her co-ordination by volunteering her to babysit with a neighbour – not much money in it, but a few regular quid for doing homework, in the same house as a sleeping baby, was fine by Jamie.

There was a chance of adding on another neighbour too, although this would mean actual children, a four-year old and a six-year-old. Perhaps she should practise on Ryan's Year 7 pupil.

The ear-rings glinted again. Perhaps she should get her ears pierced, like Kelly's, or even her nose. She winced. No, not a nose-stud. Maybe belly. She heard her own name, felt her Mum and Naomi's attention and jumped. At this rate, ace reporter Jamie Williams would have very little to report to undercover agent Ryan Anderson.

"Are you listening Jamie?" her mother's voice sharpened.

Jamie smiled brightly. "Yes."

"Naomi's going to do a reading for you, so, you sit here." Her Mum stood, and left Jamie the chair directly facing the clairvoyant across the table. Jamie sat. In front of her, upside down, were astrological charts of the kind she and Ryan had been using, or abusing, depending on how you looked at it.

"So, Jamie, tell me your birthday," Naomi began, her voice sweet and soothing, a useful voice for babysitting Jamie thought, wondering if she could copy it.

Apparently, the date alone was not exact enough, but Jamie's Mum chipped in, "Three in the afternoon, and not a moment too soon, I was sweating like a pig, and work? My body has never worked so hard–"

"Mum!" Jamie cut her off, reddening. "Too much information."

"Why don't you let Jamie and me get to know each other?" Naomi suggested, earning a grateful look.

"I wouldn't mind a look round – if you're sure you'll be all right on your own, Jamie?"

What, when I get told I'll die at seventeen, or have ten children, or something. "I'll be fine," Jamie assured her mother, wondering if she could sneak out a pen and paper, and make notes under the table, then reluctantly deciding against it. Ryan was right; they needed one of those mini-recorders or dictaphones. He'd asked his mother for one as a Christmas present, but she didn't trust him not to use it in school, to get teachers into trouble.

"How childish," he'd told her, saying later to Jamie, "Good fun, though. Can you imagine if we got the Terminator going nuclear, or Jonesie and Mair-Art having one of their *very* private chats."

"If we look at the position of the planets at the time of your birth, Mercury is particularly interesting," Naomi began, and from then on it was all very predictable, and in many ways less inspired than Ryan's readings in the school playground. Jamie was conscious of background murmurings around the room, of people shuffling in chairs.

What makes people pay for this? Jamie wondered, but then Naomi came out with, "You often feel awkward, clumsy…"

Jamie couldn't help the instinctive, "Yes."

Naomi said nothing, and Jamie continued, "It used to be worse. From when I was about eleven, I felt like I banged into things all the time or dropped them."

Silvery glints nodded sympathetically. Naomi pointed at the track of a planet on her chart, "You can see all that confusion here, with Mars opposing Neptune, but you are changing things, taking control, and this rising conjunction of Saturn and Pluto helps you.

You will look back on this as a time of great change. You are already stronger, and you will grow in confidence. But I see a shadow here. Is there something worrying you?"

Honest green eyes held Jamie's, and she suddenly ached to tell the truth, knowing that she couldn't.

"Yes," Jamie hesitated. "It's about someone else… I want to help and I don't know how."

Naomi looked again at the charts. "Someone close to you…"

Jamie nodded.

"In your family…"

Another nod.

"Older than you, so you can't tell them what to do…".

"Yes. I just can't get through to her," Jamie confessed.

"Problems… problems… perhaps related to a couple, a marriage?"

"Perhaps," Jamie sighed.

"You must remember, Jamie, that the stars tell us what we are and what might happen, but we choose our own fates and can work with the stars to make the best of our lives. You are important to… this other person – she loves you."

Jamie choked, and couldn't say anything.

"This will help her come through her problems. You are already doing so much more than you know, so much more – I see these problems rumbling around like a storm that never breaks, for a few months more, then the storm will go, the problems will be resolved."

"But is that good?" asked Jamie.

"I see happiness… happiness for you and the person you are worried about. The advice to you here is clear – just keep being yourself, showing that you care, and let this person work things through."

"Thank you," Jamie said, meaning it.

Naomi moved the charts to one side. "Let me explain

something to you, Jamie. The true gift is inside, not in the charts, not," she gestured around the room at the other psychics, "not in the cards or the t'ai chi. These are only the ways we reach our gift, ways to express the knowledge we have when we read someone, like I'm reading you now. I can see the aura around you, Jamie, and the only word I have for it is *silver*."

She thought, then added, "Quicksilver – mercury, the most amazing of elements. Always changing…I see lots of changes."

So, I'm the most amazing of elements. The thought was not unpleasant.

"I feel something special about you Jamie. Have you ever felt something strange–?"

Oh, yes. "I don't know what you mean."

"Give me your hand."

Jamie automatically held out her left hand, turned palm up for Naomi to study.

She smiled at Jamie. "Strong heart line here, and, see that?" Naomi traced one small, deep line in the side of Jamie's hand, just below her little finger. "You will have one partner, one deep love."

She gave Jamie the benefit of another clear gaze. "I know it sounds unlikely but I really do see a tall, dark man in your life."

"Very dark?" Jamie asked, trying not to giggle. She caught a glimpse of Ryan peering at crystals and reading their labels.

Naomi shrugged, then suddenly became very intent and quiet. "This," she said, "I was sure of it and here's the proof."

Jamie's hand looked much the same to her as it always had.

"The line of intuition!" Naomi's voice was still low but triumphant. "You have the gift."

Jamie felt suddenly chilled.

"You know, don't you. Something happened… you knew something before it happened."

Jamie tried to pull her hand free but the psychic's grip was surprisingly strong and firm.

"Don't be afraid, let me finish… yes, you have the gift, and your past lives are strong in you… one in particular… I can see her in you, I can hear her name… Gwenllian, Princess Gwenllian."

Jamie tugged her hand free, and shook it to get rid of the feeling that it didn't belong to her, that it was dirty.

"Don't be afraid," the gentle voice repeated, "she guides you, Princess Gwenllian, she calls to you, she is your spirit guide."

"I think that's enough now." Jamie's voice stuttered a bit, but she was recovering quickly. She could hear the sounds in the room again, she could see an old stain on the cuff of the white blouse, and she could see through this Naomi person.

She could definitely see through her.

"Yeah, well, thanks," she said.

"Remember, Jamie, your left hand is what you're born with, and your right hand shows what you make of it. Use your gift, find your way of expressing it, but don't waste it."

Jamie laughed. "I'm left-handed," she said.

Naomi shook her head. "Makes no difference."

Oh, yes, it does and I proved it a year ago, Jamie told herself, remembering all that she and Ryan had discovered about left-handers, but she said nothing as she left her chair to the next, eager client.

She could hear Naomi already speaking of Venus and 'trine', whatever that was, while she scanned the room for her mother and her friend, wondering what the hell she was going to say to either of them.

Ryan glanced across at Jamie, who seemed intent on whatever psychobabble the pretty psychic was giving her. He was amazed at what a good actress his friend was; anyone would swear that she believed every word she was being told, the way she was leaning forward, frowning in concentration, and lost to the world around her. If he could just hover near enough to hear what was being said – but no, he could trust her to tell him the details afterwards, and then they'd have fun writing up what a load of crap this all was.

"Are you here to mess about or do you actually want to learn something?" Ryan jumped at the best evidence he'd had so far of mind-reading, and he gave his best, 'Sorry I'm late, Sir,' smile, the one that usually worked in school.

The woman's glare softened a bit, and she rearranged a couple of the crystals on her stall. "You paid to come in, so I'll treat you like anyone else as long as you behave that way. At the moment, you're putting off my other clients and doing nothing yourself, so sit, or go."

Ryan sat. Sometimes the truth seemed like a good idea. "I'm doing an article for the school newspaper about the paranormal and I came here for research. Do you mind if I ask you a few questions?"

"I suppose not. As long as you have an open mind and don't come out with all those prejudiced stereotypes – you know, Gypsy Rosalie and such."

"Of course not." Sometimes a *little* bit of truth seemed quite enough. "I'm very open-minded. Do you mind if I take notes?"

"Be my guest, but make it quick. There are people here who need to see me, and aren't just nosing."

"They come to see you about–?"

"–what crystals can do for them."

She indicated the glittering displays. "You can harness the earth forces, if you know how, strengthen your own aura with your birthstone," and she pointed to a card that partnered each zodiac sign with a gemstone, "and you can create an atmosphere in a room by choosing the right stone. Suppose you want peace, a restful feel to help you sleep at night, you need malachite."

She picked up an amethyst and smoothed it. "This works with the Chakras, very good against nightmares. Or if you want to dim the lights, put on some smoochy music and get a special someone into the mood, rose quartz is the thing – I sell a lot of those."

"I'll, er, bear that in mind, Miss? Mrs?" Ryan muttered.

"Annie, call me Annie." Annie looked at him, considering. "Luck," she stated. "People need good luck for some special event like a job interview, or like an exam. Do you have some sort of lucky mascot?"

Ryan was shaking his head and didn't look up from his note-taking.

"Or something that you always do, during exams, for luck?"

Ryan paused. "I always have three black fineliners, exactly the same make, but that's just practical – no, I can't think of anything. I underline my name three times before I start, and then I just get on with it."

Annie was nodding, "So you have your routines, don't you. I think you really could be a crystal person. Something drew you to this stall – you're attracted to crystals aren't you?"

"As a matter of fact, I am." Ryan's pen paused in mid-air. "They reckon that there might be a perfect crystal right at the very inner core of the earth,"

"Quartz," Annie nodded.

"No, iron," Ryan told her, "and I've just been researching sugar and it's amazing. Did you know its properties are so similar to glass that they use sugar in film stunts – they make sugar windscreens and bottles and suchlike, so that, when they smash them, there's less danger of someone getting hurt. Looks just like the real thing. And this Venetian bloke made a whole meal out of sugar: fake meat, fake fruit, even fake cutlery and plates, so everything looked brilliant and then just crumbled – magic!"

"Magic," Annie agreed, "and you don't have to take my word for it, you can be as objective as you like, and you'll see how much better you feel with the right crystal. This is the one for you, I feel it... you're Scorpio, aren't you."

"No, Pisces."

"Ah yes, it was the water sign I could sense... and probably you are on the borders of Pisces..."

"No, smack in the middle on dates."

"There are other kinds of borders... I think Jupiter was weak at your birth."

Well my mother certainly was, Ryan restrained himself from saying, making furious notes along the lines of *'gets it wrong, changes tack, doesn't ever admit getting it wrong'*. He was glad his handwriting was so bad that even he couldn't always read it, so there was no chance of Annie making out what he was writing, upside-down.

"Lapis lazuli," Annie was holding out a chip of pinkish rock, with streaks of brightest blue on its surface. "Wear this under your shirt for luck on special occasions like exams. But not all the time," she cautioned, "or it will overpower your natural amethyst, even add an aphrodisiac tinge, which you don't need." Ryan kept his head well down and said nothing.

Then Annie held up his birthstone, a tiny raw-edged glimmer of violet. "I should have known – that's why I kept touching the amethyst when you arrived. Your natural state is relaxed and meditative. An amethyst can cure headaches and stabilize the body energies. But for exams, you need the extra adrenalin rush."

"Tell me about it."

Five minutes later, Ryan was walking away from Annie's stall, telling himself that it was purely for experimental purposes. He could feel the faint knock of an amethyst 'dragon's egg', its raw side against the newly curling hair on his chest and the polished oval face smooth against his T-shirt. And if he put his hand in his pocket, he could curl his fingers around the lapis lazuli. Jamie was still being jabbered at, so, after flicking through a book on Feng Shui and one on hypnosis, he joined the group waiting for a free show.

BIRTHSTONES

Aries	Bloodstone
Taurus	Sapphire
Gemini	Agate
Cancer	Emerald
Leo	Onyx
Virgo	Cornelian
Libra	Peridot
Scorpio	Aquamarine
Sagittarius	Topaz
Capricorn	Ruby
Aquarius	Garnet
Pisces	Amethyst

CHAPTER 7

"That's not mind-reading, that's body language." Ryan leaned over the railings that curved along the prom. He looked out across the sweep of Swansea Bay, without noticing the plumes of smoke or the ferry vanishing in the distance. The breeze was still wintry as it hit his face, making the tips of his ears tingle. A wayward gust twisted a seagull up and out to sea, like a scrap of paper dancing on a current of air.

"Right," Jamie responded, "so how did we know when to look at each other, and what exactly is the body language for "Let's get out of here and meet up across the road on the prom?""

"Easy." Ryan grinned, shrugged his shoulders, and jerked his head.

"A real winner in *Three Little Words*, I don't think," Jamie told him, but she smiled anyway. "And you know it's true, we think the same things sometimes. Maybe telepathy does exist."

Ryan appeared to consider the matter.

"No," he was definite. "There's no reason to think so. Of course, friends are going to think alike, that's why they're friends, and coincidences are bound to happen. Then people who want to believe in weird stuff get excited about the coincidences and ignore all the times nothing happened. That's what they're all doing in there, all those women." He jerked his head at the hotel they had just left, its shabby façade merging into the row of Aberafan guesthouses that had seen better days, when the beach had attracted the miners and factory workers on their day trips.

Jamie bit back a retort. He was right: it *was* all women in there. Why? She spoke the thought aloud.

"Don't ask me." Ryan took out his notebook. "I thought I'd have all kinds of answers but I'm just more confused. Apart from the way everyone left three seats empty all round me in case I was contagious."

"Well you're definitely not a woman…"

"And the way the psychic in charge of the demo glared at me, like she really wanted me to leave–"

"See, that's proof she could read your mind."

"They just don't like kids at things, it's the same if you're queuing to buy bread or whatever, you get ignored, or you get treated like you're about to steal the takings from the till."

"Same if you try to buy tickets for something, like when Kelly's singing at the Club. Anyway, what was in the demo?"

"That's what I don't get. It was so phoney, but no one seemed bothered, as if they were so keen to believe it that Mystic Maureen could have said anything to them. I wrote down some bits, here… A woman from the audience volunteered to have a reading."

"Do you think it was fixed?"

"No, I don't think so." Ryan laughed wryly. "If it was fixed, it would have been better. There's a special voice they all use, sort of dreamy and gentle. And in the demo, there were comments like, "You find it difficult to juggle the demands of others… your family… but you are so strong inside, so caring, they rely on you and you will come through for them." Sometimes she would pause, make a little guess, like "your family" and if she got nods she'd know she was warm and keep going, if she got headshaking, she'd just try another tack. But the woman being read was beaming as if she'd just got 4 A grades at A level."

Reluctantly, Jamie admitted, "I think my Mum would have liked being told things like that."

"What about your Mum, then, and what about your reading?" Jamie's stomach lurched. Friends told each other everything, didn't they? Ryan had given her all the details about crystals and they'd laughed together at the so-called healing powers of these little chips of rock. Jamie couldn't imagine anyone being daft enough to buy something like that for 'aura enhancement' and, of course, Ryan agreed with her. Someone moronic enough to wear a crystal for its magic probably still believed in the tooth fairy. So why couldn't she laugh with Ryan over what Naomi had said to her?

"Oh, there was one more thing," Ryan flicked through his

notes. "In the introduction to the demo, old witchy Maureen said, "The most difficult thing for those of us with the skill," he put on a spooky voice, "is to interpret what comes to us as a feeling, especially if it is something sad or even tragic. I had to tell one young woman that there would be some crisis, and after that she would never see her boyfriend again.

Of course, she was upset at the thought that they would break up and that's what I thought too, but she came back to visit me, two years later… I say 'visit', not 'see' because she had completely lost her eyesight, through diabetes. It had come true. She would never see her boyfriend again but he was still with her and they were about to get married." I think she believed in what she was saying, even if it was rubbish."

"That's horrible." Jamie shuddered. *Fire*, she thought, remembering her premonition about Kelly, *knowing how to interpret what comes to you as a feeling.*

"Just a story," Ryan dismissed it cynically.

"It was weird to have so much attention, all about me, and what I'm like, and what I can do." Jamie was hesitant. "Like having a bright light shone in my face, a bit too much for me. And then when she said things, I couldn't help nodding if I thought it was true."

"What sort of things?"

"Oh, you know, like me being shy but getting over it."

"A bit like the demo, but I suppose more going by your age or face or–"

"–body language," she finished for him. "Your pet theory – I know. And it's like being given a compliment if they say something nice about you."

"Like what?"

"Like you're kind, or something," she evaded. No way was she going to give him the word 'quicksilver', that coated her tongue like the aftertaste of chocolate ice-cream. "So that you can imagine a more glamorous you," she offered.

Ryan threw her a suspicious glance, but she didn't give him time to challenge her.

"I'm cold." She shivered. "Let's go home."

"What, and look at the M4 instead of the sea?"

Jamie regarded the stretches of silver disappearing into a gray horizon. "It's not even proper sea," she told him, "not like Kidwelly, where my Nan lives. She calls it mud-sucking sea, with flats and spits. You can go there with me some time if you like, we can fall down a bottomless hole, and haunt the marshes forever."

"If it's bottomless, then we'll just keep falling, and we can't haunt till we're dead."

"Well, we'll die of starvation then, while we're falling, and *then* we can haunt."

"We'll die of lack of water before we die of starvation."

"It might rain on us."

"Whatever is meant to be will be, if that is our fate…"

Jamie considered this. "That's another thing. They all seem to make a big point of saying that you still make your own fate, which doesn't fit with them saying what's going to happen."

Giving Ryan a chance to discuss whether there was such a thing as fate was like throwing a bone to a dog, and they were still tugging their futures to bits when they arrived back at Jamie's house.

"Yes, but your genes do make a kind of fate."

"So does my Dad, in person, not in my genes." Jamie made a face. "If anything stops me getting to university, it will be him, not Venus in the shadow of Saturn."

She was silent a moment, peering into the gray stretch of street along which they had just walked. "Ry, I know this will sound odd, but I keep feeling like someone's following us."

"Your sixth sense at work?" Jamie winced.

"Women's intuition?" Ryan carried on teasing, not noticing her discomfort. "You'll be behind the table at the next convention, Gypsy Jamie tells your fortune. No, I don't think we're being tailed. You're not worried about that bloke, Chris, are you?"

"No, he's just a friend."

"I think he wanted more than that, judging by the songs he was writing for you."

"Maybe, but he's got a girlfriend now. She watches the band now and then, but she's not part of it, like Kelly. No, Chris is all right. I'm sure you're right, I'm being paranoid."

"See you then."

"See you." It was only later, lounging in her bedroom, that Jamie reflected over the way the conversation had not gone, rather than how it had. She had somehow *not* mentioned the strangeness she felt, the link to whatever had happened with Kelly, and most of all she had not mentioned some weird Welsh princess.

Better not, she thought, returning to the unsolved problem of her mother. She stroked her cat absent-mindedly and was rewarded with a rumbling purr. No doubt, Jamie pondered, there was another cosy mother-daughter chat in store and she had no idea how to get past her mother's beliefs.

Three days later, Ryan decided that either paranoia was contagious, or Jamie had been right in the first place. There was a strange feeling of wrongness in what flickered in and out of his vision, a small figure that kept almost appearing. Ryan ducked behind a pillar in the shopping arcade and waited.

Sure enough, a small hoodie sauntered past him, trying to look casual, head tucked down so that Ryan couldn't see the face.

The hoodie paused just past Ryan's pillar, the back of the gray fleece hood raised up and turned from side to side. A pair of glowing new, white trainers tapped the ground anxiously, and Ryan relaxed, grinning. He knew who this was, and at least the boy had got himself some trainers, even if they needed a bit of wearing in.

Some stalker, not even thinking to look behind him! Ryan moved stealthily close enough to reach out a long arm around the hoodie's neck.

"Looking for me?" The reaction was a gratifying squeal and attempted escape, attracting tuts of disapproval from passing shoppers.

One man even stopped, frowned at them and asked, "You all right, son?"

Ryan removed his arm and let the boy speak for himself.

"Just having a laugh," Sam told the man. "He's like my big brother," and he turned his deep brown spaniel eyes towards Ryan, who groaned inwardly.

What am I going to do about this puppy? he wondered.

"Well, you look after your little brother, or people will get the wrong idea!" Ryan shrugged helplessly and the man moved off in the stream of council suits and shoppers.

"That would be cool, wouldn't it? Us being brothers?"

Ryan contemplated such a fate, briefly, but thought he could be kinder to Sam if he didn't consider it for too long. "What exactly are you up to, Sam?"

"Shopping."

Ryan sighed. "Let me put it more clearly. Why are you following me? And not just today. Why have you been following me and Jamie?"

"You're my mentor."

"Do you remember our little talk, about when we *wouldn't* see each other?"

Sam was unrepentant. "Yes, but I didn't mean you to see me, so if I hadn't slipped up, that would have been all right. And anyway, it's the holidays now, and you told me to leave you alone in school, when we didn't have our," Sam lowered his voice as if they were sharing a blueprint for a nuclear invention, "our reading lesson. And," he delivered his final justification triumphantly, "I heard you and Jamie talk about having a reading, so that's bound to be good mentoring for me isn't it."

"Not that sort of reading, idiot," Ryan snapped, then felt guilty at the way Sam's face fell as he went back to his quiet voice.

"I thought there was just reading, not different kinds," he whispered.

Ryan knew just how difficult Sam was finding reading. In fact, he admired the boy's guts for persevering. Ryan wanted to help him, but it was almost impossible when all you remembered yourself about learning to read was that you could, and that books were your friends, and that computers were fast books.

There was going to be some mentor training in school, but it had been postponed until after the holidays. A lot of things to do with Mr Travis seemed a bit confused at the moment, and Ryan put it down to the new hairdo. Still, as long as Travis was still accepting their copy for *The Afan Times*, that's all that mattered to Ryan and Jamie. It wouldn't be the first time Ryan had faced a problem on his own, and this particular problem was irritating rather than dangerous. The problem looked up at Ryan, all his lonely hero-worship pleading through his eyes.

"All right, I'll tell you about it," Ryan conceded and Sam glowed with excitement. "This is Year 10 stuff really, but I think you're ready for it now. Jamie and I have a special place, and we go there for reading."

"Reading." Sam's disappointment showed but Ryan was committed now.

"Yes, reading. And yes, there's different kinds of reading. We've just been doing storybooks in school." Unconsciously, Ryan lowered his voice when he mentioned their reading lessons, "but what I like best is the Reference Section, in there," Ryan pointed up the escalator to the second story, where the glass front of Port Talbot Library offered glimpses of the book stacks and computers inside.

"The library." Sam might as well have said, 'Brussel sprouts'.

"Have you actually been in the library?" Ryan challenged.

"Well no."

"It's warm, dry, and you can find out everything about everything, even the things your Mum doesn't want you to know."

Ryan led the way, ignoring Sam's attempt to copy his way of walking, and praying that no one he knew was anywhere near the town centre that morning.

"Don't bother with the man with the moustache, he just wants tidy books and no one in here, but always smile nicely at the fat, blonde lady – she'll help you find things and show you how to get onto the computers, if you come on your own."

"On my own?"

"Yes," Ryan was firm. If he was stuck with being a role model, at least he could use it to his advantage. "On your own. I always used to come here on my own. As well as reading books, you can meet some cool people here."

"I'm not supposed to talk to strangers. My Mum says."

"But this is a library, and the rules are like in school. You can talk to someone your own age. The best thing is to hang out by the books you like, and only talk to someone else who reads them. So, if you like football, it's the football books, if you like war books, that's where you go."

"Is that how you met Jamie?"

"Yes," Ryan lied.

"I'd love to meet someone like Jamie."

"Yes, I suppose you would."

"Where exactly did you meet?"

"Forensic science," Ryan invented, thinking that was exactly where they should have met. He distracted Sam from the inevitable "What's that" by taking him to browse the graphic novels. Sam was still reluctant to consider books, for so long 'the enemy', as friends, and Ryan was searching for some extra little burst of inspiration when his hand brushed the sharp edges hidden in his pocket. He winced at the memory of Jamie's views on people who wore crystals, and his hand automatically reached for the smoothness of the dragon's egg under his T-shirt.

If Jamie found out about his crystals, he would be able to say with a clear conscience that it had been purely experimental, and the proof would be that he'd given one to Sam.

Hidden behind the stacks, Ryan took the little lapis lazuli out of his pocket and told Sam of its special powers to improve reading skills, as long as it was kept a secret, of course.

Speechless, Sam pocketed the blue crystal, and pointed with new determination to the words he was mouthing to himself as he read.

After half an hour grabbing random books from shelves, and discussing the habits of creatures ranging from killer sharks to mountaineers, Ryan felt his virtuous glow wearing thin. He obtained a promise from Sam to stop stalking, in exchange for a weekly meeting, "Not, you know, a reading lesson, but maybe we could look at books like these."

"No, not a reading lesson," Ryan agreed. He even managed to escape with a head start, leaving Sam nervously glancing around the library, but interested enough to stay a bit longer, flicking through the Guinness Book of Records.

Ryan was breathing deeply of freedom, congratulating himself on his kindness and maturity, and the fact that no one had seen him with Sam, when he heard his name.

"Ryan-oh." Short skirt, long legs, and a way of moving the combination that made you understand what Gareth saw in her, as well as that singing voice. No trace of the angel in her day-to day speaking voice though.

"Ryan," Kelly called again, as if there'd been any chance he wouldn't hear her the first time. He waited till she caught up with him, prepared for the inevitable mickey-taking over his newly acquired 'little brother'.

"I haven't told Gareth," Kelly informed him, "about Jamie being psychic."

CHAPTER 8

The bleak heathland stretched to the sheltering granite of Mynydd y Garreg. Or rather, what should have been sheltering, Jamie thought, overwhelmed with the bitterness of her betrayal. Instead they had been trapped like rats, all her brave men. With one booted foot, she nudged a gray shape, still as a boulder in a landscape covered with many such boulders.

She grunted when she saw the corpse's face, Ieuan ap Gwilym, another brave lad gone to the hereafter, gone with Morgan. Even to say his name to herself, hammered nails into what was left of her heart. How many Welshmen with him?

She tallied up the gray shapes with a practised eye, ignoring those who had hours of thirst to pass before they bled to their doom. She was beyond helping them, beyond help. She had been here before and yet she must go through it all again, and again. She must search and she must find it, and she must endure the reliving.

She calculated that there were three Norman corpses for every dead Welsh comrade – they had fought well, her men, and yet they had all died from a knife in the back, the knife of that traitor's words. Gruffydd ap Llewellyn – how little he deserved the name. May the curse of Math be on him. She spat viciously at the blood-stained earth. Without him, their plan would have worked, the Mynydd at their backs, the element of surprise.

When they'd first seen the glint of sun on armour, the Norman army already up on the Mynydd, with the advantage of the heights, they'd guessed their fate. They'd known for sure when twice their numbers charging down the scarp had split them apart like saplings, but every man had rallied to form the shield wall.

Seeing Gruffydd ap Llewellyn screeching amid the Normans, hiding behind their mass, like the runt of the litter he surely was, would have held the Welsh army firm against the Lord of Hell himself. And some had thought it was indeed Anawn, when that Norman devil, Maurice of London, came up the river from the castle, a second army at his back to complete the crab's claws that pinched them to defeat.

So many dead. What chance of finding what she sought, amongst so many dead? She must retrace her steps, it was the only way, the only chance she had.

Jamie felt suddenly more aware of her own body, or rather this body she wore like fancy dress, battle-hardened, striding across the moorland. She ached from the clash of metal against metal, and she was starting to feel the weight of her shield, slung across her back now she had no need of it. She knew it carried some dints that would make stories over a flagon around a campfire, but this time there would be no campfire.

Her hair was tight underneath a chainmail hood, and she knew that two long, golden braids were tucked into her mail waistcoat. The bruising clump against her right hip reassured her that her sword was where it should be, for one last time. There was no colour in the place of death and Jamie was grateful.

Somewhere, underneath this frozen resignation, she was feeling queasy, muttering to herself about blood and body parts that she really didn't want to think about, or see in colour, but monochrome did not protect her from nature's way with corpses.

The huge black birds were back and she knew, when one landed on a corpse, exactly which part of the body would be considered choicest, first pickings. Somewhere, deep inside herself, Jamie was heaving, but she could not turn her gaze away. Eyes, she confirmed, as the ravens started nature's way with the dead.

Seeming unmoved, Jamie scanned the field, until she found the group of the living, who must have been there all the time, so close they were. And yet it was if they had appeared from nowhere, in colour. Their ragged battle gear showed rough cloth of blue or red underneath the silver metal.

Some soldiers were still collecting and soothing loose horses, battle plunder. Another lurch of the heart as Jamie realised that her own Saeth, her 'arrow', would be among them. Norman prisoner was the best fate any of them could hope for, man or horse. Her eyes were drawn to a central figure, held between two Normans.

"No," she groaned, "must I go through this all again."

She felt the very air blur round her, heard angry shouts, disagreement and above it all, her own voice, loud and clear. "Cofiwch Gwenllian!" she shouted and then someone bent her head over, the dizziness swirled into deep retching sickness, impossible to keep down. Her stomach muscles clenched, and it was a relief to Jamie to give in, to think of nothing but voiding this bitterness inside her.

"Jamie, Jamie, for God's sake, you've got to get out of that bed." Jamie woke to a vile smell that reminded her of the reek of the battlefield and contracted her own heaving stomach once more. Her mother sounded more concerned than angry, and Jamie let herself be led to the bathroom where she lay on the floor, her head reeling and her insides gradually, mercifully settling. Her mother sat beside her on the bathroom floor, cradling her as if she were six years old again. If only, she thought, weak and confused.

"Drink a little water, love, and then, when you're feeling up to it, you'll feel better if you have a shower. I'll sort out your bedroom, and then we'll see if you're well enough to get up."

"I think I'm OK now," Jamie told her, and if 'OK' meant that she wasn't going to throw up again, then it was the truth and as much of it as she could manage for now.

An hour later, Jamie sat in the kitchen, sipping water and eating dry toast.

"Time of the month?" her mother asked.

"No, must be a stomach bug or something," Jamie told her. "Sod's law getting it in the holidays."

"How do you feel now?"

"Fine." The sort of fine where you feel you've been kicked in the head and the stomach by a really vicious horse. "Fine," she repeated.

Her mother had her back turned and was swopping dirty and clean dishes around the sink.

"Naomi told me," she said to the wall, "about you being… sensitive."

Oh God, not now. Jamie's stomach dipped like on *The Ride of Death* at Alton Towers, and she forced down another mouthful of toast.

"I want you to know I understand." *Glad someone does.* "Have you had any… feelings?"

That was easy. "No," Jamie was clear. "No, I think your friend has made a mistake." There really was no point telling her mother that it was all rubbish, not when she couldn't think straight herself. *Get a grip, girl.* Whatever weird stuff was going on, Jamie had no doubt whatsoever that her mother was being ripped off by a bunch of con-artists. She wondered how much her mother had spent at the psychic event. With a sudden pang, she realised her mother must have paid for Jamie's session with Naomi. She was making things worse, not better.

"Mrs Evans, from Number 14, was chatting at the till yesterday."

Jamie was relieved but suspicious at the change of topic and murmured a non-committal "Mm?"

Her mother continued, "She's looking for a babysitter and I said you might be interested in a bit of pocket-money, and that you were a very reliable girl, often looked after getting food ready here when I'm at work."

Jamie didn't have to feign her enthusiasm. She needed every penny she could scrounge, if she was going to get to university and survive there. "Thanks, Mum. It's a baby, is it?"

"Yes." Her Mum smiled. "And sleeping well on a night, so

it sounds like a nice little number. Not like you and Gareth."

"You've told me before." Jamie hurried her mother on. The last thing she wanted were reminiscences about what hard work she and her brother had been. That often led on to what hard work they still were. "Do I have to call her?"

"I said you'd call round. Tuesday night she wants to go out. And then, if she's happy, once a week, she said."

"Great." Jamie was already calculating how much she could put into savings.

"Jamie…"

"Hmm?"

"Women are better at this sort of thing you know…"

"Babysitting?"

"Well, that too, but I meant… instincts."

Oh no.

"I don't think your Dad and Gareth would understand about the… other world. They don't like to think about anything that they can't drink or watch on telly." Her mother laughed bitterly.

"Gareth talks about all kind of things," Jamie defended her brother.

"Maybe." Her mother shook her head. "But it's different for us women. We see things, know there's more to life."

She stopped screwing up the tea towel, plugged it into the rubber holder stuck on the wall, and turned to face Jamie.

"To be honest, I need your help, and it makes it a bit easier to ask, now that I know you have a gift. You'll understand more and more, yourself."

Why does that sound like a threat? Jamie wondered.

"And you're right about me having spent a bit more than I should have, just for the moment… but it's just cash flow. So, I wondered… I wondered if you could lend me some of your savings? Just for a bit? Of course, I'll pay you back."

Jamie swallowed. Her precious savings. Her birthday and Christmas money from her Nan. Her future. What if she said no? She knew exactly what her mother needed the money for; she'd already seen the bills. She pictured her father's face if he found out. When he found out. He wasn't a hitting man. At least, she didn't think he was a hitting man. But it turned her stomach to jelly when he shouted and shook the house, so that it still echoed with his anger, long after he'd left to walk it off, or drink it off. Then they'd all be walking around on tiptoes, almost whispering, so as not to spark him off again. Even Gareth.

Jamie's voice came out squeaky. "How much?"

Her mother didn't look at her. "Two hundred."

"How," she hardly dared ask, but she had to, "how are you going to pay it back?"

A bright smile answered her. "That's easy. In August. There's money coming my way in August, if I invest now, and keep steady in my enterprise."

Her mother hesitated. "I wish… I wish I'd done more when I was your age. Maybe, I could've stayed on in school. Gone to university, even." She gave a bitter laugh. "But your Dad came along."

The lump in Jamie's throat felt like a hippo stuck in a python but she managed, "OK," followed by "I'm feeling a bit rough again, I'll go for a lie down."

She hardly heard her mother's softly-spoken, "Thanks, Jamie," as she crashed upstairs, and onto her bed, where she watched the cat's ear twitch as a tear trickled down the soft fur.

Hunger woke Jamie, and she rubbed her cheek where the pillow had dug fold lines into her skin. She was feeling more like herself now – the phrase made her smile. Princess Gwenllian in a past life? She didn't think so. There was no way she was giving up the fight. She would not let her mother disappear into this mad world of horoscopes and false hopes; and she would not let weird coincidences, spooky talk and a scary dream get the better of her.

Raiding the fridge boosted her morale even more, and she thought about her dream. What would Ryan say? Well, obviously, that Naomi had put the idea into her head, and then all the things she knew about the old Welshies, had just mixed up into her dream. "Know your enemy," Ryan always said, so Jamie would find out who Gwenllian really was, and then she could laugh the dream away.

She had another idea to try with her mother; if rubbishing the psychic world didn't work, perhaps Jamie could use her mother's belief, now that Jamie was supposed to be 'a sensitive'. She made a face at herself in the mirror, which shimmered back at her. Quicksilver, mercury… she gave the mirror a defiant glare, and wished she had Gwenllian's sword buckled on, as she planned what she was going to tell Ryan. It was time to talk to him, properly.

"See." Jamie showed Ryan her information about the princess. "She's sad and I'm sorry for her and all that, but she's nothing like my dream. I didn't dream anything about babies and nuns, and I just know I was speaking Welsh, and you *know* my Welsh is about as good as my history."

"How do you know you were speaking Welsh?"

"It's just one of those things you know in a dream, like I knew it was black and white at first, then suddenly colour. And anyway, I remember the bit I shouted at the end, *Cofiwch*."

"That's easy, that's just 'Remember.'"

"Easy for you, maybe. I hate Welsh."

"Yeah, I know, you wouldn't know your *Hywel da* from your *boreda*."

"What's–" Jamie started to ask, "Oh, never mind, I haven't got time for a Welsh lesson."

"If you really were visiting a past life–"

"Which I wasn't–"

"We agreed that we'd think about this objectively," Ryan reminded her. "And if you were this Gwenllian, then maybe you were dreaming the battle where her father lost his head?"

"But she was a baby then, and it didn't feel like that."

"Well you could have been the adult Gwenllian, dreaming she'd gone back in time to that battle."

Jamie kept shaking her head and Ryan gave up that train of thought.

"So, you were worrying about what this Naomi said, and your subconscious threw up all kinds of things about people in the old days, that you didn't even know you knew."

"That would be hellish useful in exams, if I could get all that Welsh back into my head."

"Like all that sleep-teaching, hypnosis for revision… perhaps we can try– "

"No," Jamie was firm. "We've got enough going on without trying to get stuff up from our mental hard drives onto easy-access," which was how Ryan had explained to her the relationship between her subconscious and her conscious mind. "Anyway, we've proved that my dream was an anxiety one, nothing psychic about it at all, and we can do a piece on dreams for the next *Afan Times*. You can put in all that Freudian theory you've been coming out with."

Somewhere in England, on the B1177 road between Ponton and Billingborough, in Lincolnshire, there is a memorial to the last descendant of Welsh royal blood.

In memory of
Gwenllian
Daughter of the last Prince of Wales
Born at Abergwyngregyn 12.6.1282
Died at Sempringham 7.6.1337
having been held prisoner for 54 years

THE LAST PRINCESS
OF WELSH ROYAL BLOOD

Gwenllian's mother died giving birth to her, and her father, Prince Llywelyn the Last, was killed in the land of Bwellt by English troops. His head was sent to the Tower of London and displayed by King Edward I, to show the end of the royal line of Wales or 'Gwalia' as it was once called. From then on, 'Prince of Wales' was a title given to the King's – or Queen's – eldest son.

To make sure that baby Gwenllian had no children to threaten his control of Wales, Edward arranged for her to spend the rest of her life as a nun in the Gilbertine Priory of Sempringham, in Lincolnshire. It was only in 1993 that a memorial was erected there and, according to locals, the figure of a nun now haunts the spot.

Surrounded by only English speakers, Gwenllian didn't even know how to say or spell her own name, copying those around her and calling herself 'Wentlyann'.

"OK, but," Ryan hesitated, "what about the thing with Kelly?" He found it difficult to say what Kelly had told him, and Jamie realised that it was not just her apparent prophecy that troubled him but his own memories. Anything that involved a gun, even an air gun, reminded him of the year before, and of how desperately wrong things could go.

"Kelly is convinced you saved her from getting shot," he said.

Jamie scoffed, keeping up her sceptical façade. "Kelly would believe in anything. Have you seen her desks during exams? She has more lucky charms than I have freckles – not that they do her any good."

"But what about you, the fact you said something, and then it turned out to be true? Like that story the psychic told in the demo."

Jamie admitted, "I did wonder. That's probably been part of the worry that triggered the dream, and the feeling sick, like when someone spins you till you're dizzy, and you think you're falling, but you're not. We were reading about horo-scopes and all these psychic phenomena, you were reading cards, and it starts to get your brain whirring so you imagine things."

"But it did come true."

"It's what you've always said, that if you keep making predictions, some will come true, just by coincidence and by *interpretation.*" She emphasised the word sarcastically. "That's just a way of giving more chances of something *seeming* like it's come true. I mean, I wasn't thinking of an air gun, was I.

I was thinking of matches and flames, so it didn't come true because it wasn't what I imagined at all. When you think about it, it took two weeks for something to happen, anything at all, and then it was nothing like I predicted, so it was typical of what these psychics do – a load of crystal balls!"

It felt like such a weight off her mind to say it, to believe it. "And some of them might even believe they have this 'gift' but that doesn't make it true."

"So, Gypsy Jamie," Ryan teased her, "what are we doing about your mother?"

"Where's your cards?" asked Jamie.

Ryan produced a pack.

"Right, let's go over the layout and the meanings again. I want to sound like you." Jamie grinned at him. "But better."

CHAPTER 9

WHAT ARE DREAMS?

There have been many theories over the centuries:

* visits from the gods or God, to pass on prophecies, warnings or plans.

* visits from demons or evil spirits, possessing you

* predictions of what is going to happen

* the intrusion of real stimuli into sleep

LOUIS ALFRED MAURY, a 19th C Frenchman, wrote down what he had dreamed after servants had carried out his instructions:

* when he was tickled with a feather on his lips and nose, while he was asleep, he dreamed of his face being tortured

* when a hot iron was held near his face, he dreamed that robbers had broken into the house and were forcing people to give up their money, by pushing their feet into hot fires.

* your subconscious (parts of your brain at work without you being aware of it) dealing with your daytime problems, worries, hopes and fears

* the brain entertaining itself while you are asleep, replaying events and making up stories, like watching a TV soap

* a way of rehearsing for dangerous situations

* self-expression

FREUD, an Austrian Jew who is thought of as the Father of Psychology, wrote "The Interpretation of Dreams". He thought dreams were all about wishes, often subconscious ones:

* a wish coming true

* a wish coming true, but disguised as something else

* a wish you don't admit you have, coming true, disguised as something else

* a wish from when you were little, coming true, disguised as something else

So, as far as Freud was concerned, everything meant something else; if you dreamed about winning the lottery, it probably meant you were scared of your father!

Everyone dreams but not everyone remembers dreaming.

Scientists have worked out that when you dream, your eyelids twitch a lot, known as R.E.M. (Rapid Eye Movement). If you don't get the type of deep sleep in which you dream, you don't feel properly rested and you start to feel ill, so we know that, whatever the reason, you need dreams for mental health.

The part of the brain that dreams also controls motivation. If this part of the brain is damaged, people can follow instructions but do nothing of their own accord.

WHAT DO YOUR DREAMS MEAN?

Start your own psycho-analysis; keep a dream diary and compare notes with your friends.

If you dream that:

∗ you are starkers when everyone else is wearing clothes,

this is often a sign of anxiety about something. You are worried about being shown up, or making a fool of yourself. People get this dream before an interview, before performing in public — or after such an event.

∗ of being chased,

then you are worried about something or someone but not facing up to it. Some people can control their dreams enough to turn around and face whatever is chasing them in the dream, and this can have a positive effect in their daytime lives. Others might work out in daytime whatever it is that "chasing" them, and find a daytime way of sorting it out.

∗ of finding treasure,

it is a sign that you are ready for change, for a new adventure, perhaps for trying again something that you tried before, whether it worked that time around, or not

* of an accident,

unless you have been in an accident, and are reliving it to get it out of your system, it could be a premonition of something bad coming. Often your subconscious is aware of risks that you are taking and will warn you in this way.

* of strange buildings,

these often represent you, so that you might be exploring different ways of looking and being with others. Ask yourself how you feel about the building — comfortable? put off? admiring? really keen to get into it and have a look around? — then apply those feelings to how you feel about your own body and daytime self.

* of falling,

this is sometimes triggered by the feeling of 'falling' asleep, or shifting from one mode of consciousness to another, and often wakes a person up.

It could also be a sign of anxiety.

* of flying,

like falling, this can be a sign of changing from one state of consciousness to another. It can also be an adventure, an exciting exploration of something new, with a feeling of freedom.

* certain symbols - a tiger, a flashy car, a snake...

As far as Freud was concerned, dreams were about wishes, wishes were about sex, and most symbols came down to sex — even dreaming about sex was about sex.

Other psychologists are a bit less obsessed with sex and have found that different people have different symbols and stories that seem to represent certain events or feelings. Ask yourself what you felt about the person or thing in your dream.

TELL ME ABOUT THE SNAKE AGAIN

Many people will read certain symbols the same way because they have the same cultural background. For people coming from cultures with a Christian background, the snake represents temptation, evil and (of course) sex. For people in some other cultures the snake represents healing and it is for this older meaning that the insignia of the British Royal Army Medical Corps show a serpent.

Then again, for someone who has been bitten by a snake, or who keeps a python as a pet, there might be a more personal interpretation of a dream snake.

Dreams sometimes pick up on puns and wordplay too, so a combination of a python and the dreamer being naked could represent the full Monty (Python), and be a variation on the traditional anxiety dream of being in the nude when others are all clothed.

This time, Jamie could look on the battlefield without her head reeling. She knew she must find it, however often she had to return to do so, and she scanned the scene, forcing her gaze away from the twisted faces of open-eyed corpses, men she knew so well. She could do nothing for them now, could not close their eyes nor wish them Godspeed to the hereafter, let alone give them the warriors' send-off they deserved, with fire and feasting. Was that a glitter over there? She trailed through the mud, and blood-stained clumps of grass, where boots had tramped and turned, their owners finally trapped.

She schooled herself to feel nothing, hear no sounds, be all searchlight. She steadied herself mentally, her left hand resting by habit on her scabbard, ready to draw her sword. Her long strides carried her towards the glint, around obstacles, human or natural, without stopping. Thank the gods that there was no smell, although some part of her mind knew exactly what the smell *would* be: that mix of sweat, blood and the bodily outcomes of fear and death.

Once more, she forced her thoughts away from such a track. Time to search was always short and she was so drawn, against her will, to where – again, she forced her thoughts away from that place, to the glitter. She hurried to spot, hoping – and found that the sunlight had caught a coin.

A coin! She kicked it over with the toe of her boot. As

much use to her as to its dead owner, his hand flung out as if reaching after the contents of his little leather pouch. The coin glittered again, mocking her. What right had the sun to shine on such a day! With Morgan dead, defending her. Jamie stumbled and shivered.

As if flung across the sky, swirling clouds blackened the sun, chilling this landscape of the dead, calling her to join her men. "Morgan," she breathed, suddenly poised beside a young man's body, his hair the same sweep of shiny brown his father's had once been, his face the same sweet baby's she'd rocked to sleep.

She crooned a lullaby to herself, her own baby-song, composed once upon a time for the new princess by Meilyr, the most famous bard Ynys Môn had ever known.

"*Sleep little princess, an apple rose-cheeked in your hand*," she sang, but even in Meilyr's words, her fathers and brothers struck for Gwalia against the Normans. Always at war. Even as a baby, this princess had no choice that would not lead here, to this southern field.

How many times could she stand this heartbreak, the scream that never ended, the fate she could not face for someone else? But she could at least face her own. The old Welsh lullaby strummed in her senses as she gave in to the maelstrom, flew with it into that group of soldiers, gathered, somber.

She flew once more into the body held pinioned, heard

the unthinkable order, the gasp of Normans and Welsh prisoners alike, saw Maelgwyn, prisoner but living. *Spared,* she thought, *at least he's spared.*

And she held herself ramrod straight, princess twice, by birthright and marriage. Her neck itched in anticipation of the sword she knew was sharp enough, thank the gods, and once again her quest ended, as she shouted her pride and challenge to the gathering winds.

"Cofiwch Gwenllian!" She fell into the words, lifted on the black winds, losing consciousness, beyond despair.

Jolted awake, Jamie lay shivering, unsure of where she was, of who she was. As she recovered her awareness of her body and her bed, she realised that her duvet had slipped off the bed. No wonder she was so cold, and that shivering had slipped into her dream. Switching on the light, she forced herself to recall her dream, noting that it really did not fit the historical facts, so there was no need to get supernatural about it.

She would discuss her subconscious with Ryan, who would no doubt enjoy playing interpreter. He had really taken to the analysis of dreams. Like Charlie getting to the chocolate factory, she thought, a boy who'd never had any himself getting the chance to glut on other people's.

She corrected herself. Of course Ryan dreamed, or he'd have mental problems. He just didn't remember them.

She thought about Ryan. On second thoughts, perhaps he *didn't* dream. Thinking about Ryan distracted her enough to ignore a haunting sense of loss, and to relax back into a deep, dreamless sleep.

She had been right about Ryan's enjoyment of her dream. "Why do I feel I've got to find something?"

"It's probably how you feel about your life, like you're finding yourself at the moment, or choosing what you want to do in the future – I bet you still haven't filled in that Careers form, have you?"

"No," Jamie admitted.

"And what you say was the worst bit is dead easy. That bit we read about Gwenllian's father having his head cut off must have stuck in your mind, and you just put it into the story your brain is telling you."

"You're probably right." Jamie sighed. "But I really don't want to keep dreaming this stuff."

"Hey, you should be glad Freud isn't analysing your dream."

"Why?"

"Dreams about getting your head cut off are all about castration worries and penis envy."

"You what!" Jamie flushed crimson but Ryan seemed oblivious to her embarrassment.

"According to Freud, all women are miserable because they haven't got a penis, and men are all scared that what women really want is to cut off their penises."

"That is the daftest thing I've ever heard. And they've never mentioned it once in sex education lessons in schools."

Ryan thought about that. "They probably don't want to give you girls ideas."

Jamie made a swipe at him.

"See," he told her, "you're starting already."

"You've got a customer," Jamie told Ryan, nodding towards a classmate, who was nervously shifting from one foot to another, waiting for a chance to speak.

"I read your article in *The Afan Times* and they said you're collecting people's dreams, and explaining them…" The boy kept his eyes fixed on the floor as he spoke, "but I don't want anyone to know about what I'm telling you." Jamie and Ryan exchanged glances.

"I'm off anyway," Jamie told him.

"It's like for doctors," Ryan explained kindly. "It's all confidential."

"I know." The boy's face brightened. "The Official Secrets Act."

"Well, actually," Ryan started, but saw the changing expression. "Yes," he said, "yes. And you've been dreaming…?"

"That I'm a gorilla. And I crunch things up when I walk

round, because I'm mega-big, as high as a multi-story, and really strong. But I'm not a proper gorilla because…"

"Because…?" Ryan prompted, scribbling furiously in his notebook.

"What are you writing down?"

"It's all right, it's all anonymous."

"Oh well that's all right, then."

"Because…? Ryan prompted again.

The boy whispered, "because I'm wearing pink fluffy slippers with *a little pony* on them."

"Ah," said Ryan.

"What's anonymous mean anyway?"

Ryan sighed. This was going to be a long but deeply interesting session. He wondered what Freud's views on the gorilla dream would have been. He wondered if Freud's theories would have been different if he'd gathered his ideas on mental health from mentally healthy people, instead of those who were mentally ill. He contemplated the specimen in front of him, and wondered what 'mentally healthy' *meant* exactly, and then he began his response.

Jamie selected the queen of clubs. "Dark-haired woman, fire sign," she told her mother. "That's you."

"I know that." Her mother twisted on the kitchen chair, impatient.

Jamie held her breath for a beat, willed herself into the part she must play, replaced the queen in the pack and shuffled the deck. She would be quicksilver, mercurial, a not-Jamie. She had to gain her mother's trust, but surely that would be easy enough. After all, her Mum had fallen for every word of who-knows-how-many con-artists on the telephone. She'd been willing enough to try out Jamie's 'gift', once Dad and Gareth were out of the house.

"Think of what it is you want to know," Jamie told her mother, then laid an eight-card spread, dropping into the manner that she had practised with Ryan, her voice soft and cool, professional. She turned over the cards, one at a time, starting with the bottom left, indicating the body or material circumstances.

"Seven of clubs," she mused. "You are determined to do something, to go ahead with a project, to change material things – even if it means you have a battle on your hands."

Jamie could feel her Mum nodding as the next card was turned over. "And this shows the emotions surrounding your question. The queen of hearts," Jamie smiled – everyone knew this one, and it was so true of her mother.

"You are so full of love, always thinking of other people, always generous... but the card is reversed... this love is causing problems in your decision."

She considered the seven of clubs again. "And if you take the two cards together there is a real clash between what you want for yourself and the way you feel about other people."

"Yes," her mother interrupted, "that's just how it is. Go on, Jamie. Tell me what I should do."

This was the moment, Jamie thought, the moment she should lead her mother away from the fortune tellers, into some healthy scepticism. She could make up something funny, something to break the spell. It didn't matter what the next card was, she could say whatever she wanted and her Mum would believe her. She was totally hooked.

Jamie tingled with concentration, the air electric as she reached for the third card. "The jack of diamonds," she breathed. Now was the moment, she could even make the card work for her.

"Hard-working," she started, "no shortcuts… the only way to get there is by hard work…" *not by some mystic razzle-dazzle*, she was going to say, but then she saw it, the combination of cards, and she couldn't do that to her mother. She couldn't make the cards lie.

Her voice shook a little as she said, "With the queen, the jack makes a special pair, a special relationship. The queen is the adult, the jack the young person, the teenager… it's the young one who's reversing the queen, who's trying the love of the adult, who's making this decision so difficult, who's against you, blocking you."

"Adult and teenager," her Mum repeated, "like—"

"Yes," Jamie said quietly, "like mother and child." She didn't have to try any more to remember the meanings of the cards. They read themselves in front of her, showing her all her mother's doubts and longings, her desire to do right by her family, and her growing dissatisfaction with her own life. Coolly, neutrally, Jamie told her Mum what she saw, lost in untangling this life she could see in the cards.

"And the last one is," Jamie turned over the card, "the two of diamonds, the juggler, reversed."

She looked back over the spread, considering the adjacent jack of spades with its warning to face facts, and she concluded. "You have to juggle, keep on juggling, what you want against what others want, your job and the money it brings, against what you want for the future, but you can adapt, others can adapt — they won't make your juggling easy – that's the reversal – but," she pointed back to the seven of clubs, "that's where the determination comes in."

She looked straight at her Mum, suddenly exhausted. "Go for it, Mum," she told her.

"Oh Jamie, thank you." Jamie didn't feel like she deserved the big hug that followed. She had been more deserving of the jack of diamonds. Her Mum smoothed down her rumpled shirt, and rose from her chair decisively. "That is such a help. Now I know exactly what to do. Do you want a cup of tea, love?"

"Please," Jamie answered, wondering what the hell she had done.

CHAPTER 10

"Don't worry about it," Ryan told Jamie. "If your Mum trusts you for a reading, that will stop her spending money on other people, so that solves the biggest problem. And, to be honest, I don't really think we're going to change her ideas, whatever we prove – I don't understand it."

"I know. But," Jamie had shared enough with her friend to blurt out the rest, "at this rate, I'll end up as loopy as she is." She shifted slightly so that the table wobbled underneath her. They were in a corner of a designated 'wet day classroom'.

Ryan considered this. "No," he finally decided, "no way, because you don't believe it's magic, or that you're magic."

Jamie opened her mouth to object but he cut her off.

"I know, you're going to say, but what about the way you felt when you were reading the cards?"

Jamie nodded.

"I said you're not magic, not that you have no talent."

If Ryan noticed the colour rushing to Jamie's cheeks, he showed no sign of it, his brow furrowed as he developed his thoughts. "All I'm saying is that there's a rational explanation, as if, when you concentrate on the cards, it opens up your mind more – I mean, they say you only use five per cent of your brain so there's lots in there that we don't know about – and all these things you know subconsciously, come through when you talk about the cards. After all, you know loads about your mother, but maybe don't really think about her life until you concentrate on the cards."

"Maybe," Jamie conceded.

"Definitely. And to tell you the truth, I feel the same way about dreams. When I did the card readings, I was just making it all up from the books, but when people are telling me their dreams, the possible meanings just seem so clear to me, I don't understand why they can't see it themselves in the first place. I don't see what's wrong with you reading cards for your mother – or for Kelly, seeing as she keeps asking you. Have you filled in that Careers questionnaire yet?"

Jamie sighed, "No."

"Well, I know now, what I want to do."

"Does that mean you've given up on being a rocket scientist, archaeologist and Prime Minister?"

"Kids' stuff," Ryan dismissed his previous life goals. "Anyway, I can't compete against you for Prime Minister. I'd rather support your campaign – as usual."

She smiled. "OK, so what this time? Journalist?"

He acknowledged the hit. "I've thought about it, despite following in Mom's footsteps." He used the word 'Mom' as if holding it with tweezers. "But I know what I want now, for sure. I'm going to become a psychologist."

"What, be round psychos all the time?"

"That's psychiatrists."

"Same difference."

"No, it isn't."

Jamie dismissed the distinction. "Anyway, *Doctor*, looks like you've got a client," and she added under her breath, "and I reckon he might use one per cent of his brain, on a good day."

A small figure was fighting his way towards them through huddles of pupils, some still dirty and dripping from playing the usual wet play routines, like 'push your friend under the gutter-spout', or 'splat his coat with mudballs'.

"Oh, no," Ryan had time to mutter before summoning up an ambiguous 'What do you want and don't be too long about it', kind of smile. At least that's what Ryan hoped his face said, but Sam was as good at reading faces as he was at reading fantasy novels, so you never knew what he had understood. "Sam…"

The Year 7 pupil plumped himself onto the table beside Jamie, forcing her to occupy an uncomfortable corner. Having commandeered one of the few chairs available, Ryan found he was in the unusual situation of looking up to his – what was he exactly? If Ryan was the mentor, was Sam a mentee? mented? De-mented, perhaps.

Sam launched into a speech that he delivered at top speed, "I know you said for me not to bother you except at the times we said but I've got a dream and everyone says it's OK to come and tell you dreams so that's all right then, isn't it?"

I have a dream, brothers and sisters, Ryan thought ruefully, having just studied Martin Luther King, and suffered knowing, supportive looks from the Citizenship teacher all the way through the lesson. By the end of it, he could have cheerfully shot the oh-so-perfect black rights activist personally.

No, not shot. He winced. Even in fun, he could not think those words. But still, he could wish some of the teachers knew more, or worried less, about black role models. He grinned with real sympathy at Sam, who had all this ahead of him.

"OK, so what's this dream?"

"Well, my mother's yelling 'Come on then Sam, come on then, you can do it'."

Ryan was writing furiously. "This is in the dream?"

"I said so, didn't I?" Sam was indignant but admitted, "But she has said that, in real life, too."

"Hmm. Go on…"

"And she wants me to go flying. I look out the window and there she is, flying around the place and going 'wheee' like she's on a ride at Alton Towers or something, and she's wearing a skirt, which is a stupid idea when you're going flying, and I don't like the idea that these people can see up her skirt, but I'm not going to have her saying I'm a chicken, so then I jump out the window, and I'm flying, but she's always going higher and higher, so I can't catch up, and then I get scared, and start falling and falling… and I don't like it," Sam finished lamely.

"Classic." Ryan chewed the end of his pen for a minute, watched by Sam and Jamie. They'd been leaning towards each other to be heard over the hubbub of what felt like hundreds of kids crammed into the room.

When he spoke, his voice was heavy with responsibility. "Someone's got to tell you, Sam, so it might as well be me. First you need to understand that it's quite normal to have these feelings. It's a stage every boy goes through, according to Freud, and I think he's right about this."

"Is he a teacher?" asked Sam.

Ryan hid a smile. Of course, Sam wouldn't have read *The Afan Times* – perhaps they'd look at it in their next reading lesson – it would be more fun than some of the books he was supposed to choose from. "No, he's a doctor who knows lots about dreams. He wrote a book about it."

"Oh, well he must know lots, then. So, what does it mean?"

"It means you've got an Oedipus Complex." Ryan was conscious that Jamie was watching him wide-eyed, mouthing "no" but it didn't do to hide things. Mom had told him often enough that if someone was old enough to ask the question, then he was old enough to get a truthful answer. Ryan just wished she'd waited sometimes until he asked the question. But Sam was not four, and this was not about his father being a sperm bank.

"Is that like a leisure complex?" Sam was looking puzzled.

"No, this sort of complex is a kind of worry, and this particular worry is named after a story about this bloke Oedipus, but you don't have to know all that. All you need to know is that you've got the same worry as this Oedipus."

"So, he had the same dream." Sam was reassured at figuring it out.

"Sort of," Ryan hedged. "So, it means you want to have sex with your mother."

"Gross," Sam flinched away from Jamie, and his disgust was written all over his face.

"That's what the flying is all about, and you want to kill your father so you can take his place with your mother."

"But I haven't seen my father since I was a baby."

"And that's why it's just the idea of people looking up your mother's skirt, possible fathers, rather than one particular person. Any of them could spoil your place with your mother."

Ryan was pleased with himself and careful to reassure Sam,

"But people don't really do these things, it's just feelings coming out in dreams, part of growing up."

Sam was bubbling spit, lost for words. When he finally regained the powers of speech, he pleaded, "You're joking, right?"

Jamie glared at Ryan, then gave Sam her warmest smile and said, "This Oedipus turned out to be a great king and he got over all these worries about his relationship with his mother. But I don't agree with Ryan. I think your dream is about you doing too much homework and it's hard, like the flying, and your mother's putting pressure on you to do better, so you're just feeling all this pressure, and it shows in your dreams."

Sam's face brightened, "Yes, that's more like it. Thanks, Jamie. But," he added hastily, unwilling to choose between his heroes. "I think your ideas are really… interesting, Ryan. This Weedypuss, was he a good reader?"

It was all Ryan could do not to jump as a hard kick found his thigh. "He was a crap reader," he began carefully, sensing the foot ready to swing again, "but he worked on it, and had one of the biggest libraries in the ancient world, so big he became famous for being a good reader – and for getting on well with his mother."

"That's all right then." Sam bounced off the table. "I want to beat the bell. See you then."

When he was well out of earshot, his analysts accused each other. "What are you trying to do to that poor boy?"

Ryan countered, "You could have wrecked my Oedipus complex for good if that kick had landed a bit to the left."

"Don't be vulgar. And anyway, you deserved it. It's like giving the kid Doctor Frankenstein for a mentor. I thought you didn't agree with Freud?"

"I think he has a point about mothers, and your interpretation can fit with mine; there's no contradiction at all. It's still an Oedipus complex."

They carried on arguing for the five minutes that older students always allowed for the classroom and corridors to clear of massed bedlam, then they made their way to their form-room, noting through the corridor window a red sports car zip into the yard where teachers parked. They paused, not recognising the car – and it was not the sort of car you forgot.

"Ah," they said in unison, as, shielding his newly blonde hair from the rain with his jacket, Mr Travis unfolded himself from the passenger seat, then leant back to the window, presumably to kiss someone hidden from view.

"Explains a lot," Jamie commented.

"Mmm," Ryan agreed comfortably, and they put their differences aside, armed with a ready and convincing excuse if they were later than their teacher for registration.

CHAPTER 11

As far as Ryan was concerned, he had already started his chosen career. He had three full notebooks and a thriving clientele for dream interpretation. His only setback had been when he asked Kelly if she'd like to tell him her dreams; she had told him where to get off and asked Jamie to check what the cards said about getting rid of weirdos.

It was during a session with the cards, which had become as familiar to Jamie as brushing her hair that Kelly suggested trying a Ouija board, and, somehow, one thing led to another so that the three of them arranged to meet up while Jamie was babysitting and they could be guaranteed some privacy.

"It's just another experiment," Ryan told Jamie, as she took a glass out of the kitchen cupboard. They'd already put the letters of the alphabet, the numbers and the *Yes/No* cards around the table in a circle, and were waiting for Kelly.

"Yes, but Kelly believes in this stuff and we're encouraging her."

"It wouldn't be a proper experiment if none of us believed in it. And it's a chance for you to hear from your spirit guide," he teased her and pretended to listen. "Oh, there she is – I'm sure I heard a baby crying."

"There had better not be," said Jamie grimly, "or you can

forget your séance. That baby never wakes up, so if she does tonight, it really will be a case of demonic possession."

There was a soft knock at the door, and Jamie let Kelly in. After all the card readings, it felt almost natural to sit together at the dining table, focused on the circle of letters. Ryan stood a torch behind them on a sideboard and switched off all the lights. Their shadows flickered like bodysnatchers, creeping along the walls with bony wavering fingers.

Jamie shivered.

"Should we hold hands?" Ryan asked innocently. Even in the dim light, Jamie could feel the sharp look Kelly sent his way.

"In your dreams," she told him sharply. "Put your finger on the glass. This one." She pointed the index finger of her right hand and the others followed suit. Jamie automatically reversed the instruction as meant for her left hand.

"Now we ask a question," Kelly told them, "and we wait to see if a spirit comes."

"Is there anyone there?" she asked, soft and low, lifting the small hairs on the back of Jamie's neck.

Nothing happened.

They waited in silence.

Jamie's arm was starting to ache with being stretched out in one position.

"Jamie, you try," Kelly said. "You're the one they talk to."

Jamie swallowed. Her voice cracked a little as she repeated the question. "Is anyone there?"

They waited again.

Then the glass gave a little jump beneath their fingers, and moved a tiny bit towards the *Yes* card, stopping when Jamie jerked her hand back as if she'd been burnt.

"Put it back," the others hissed and, slowly, she put her finger back on the glass, felt the movement, watched the glass stop in front of *Yes*.

"Go on," Kelly told her. "Ask something else."

But Jamie's mind had blanked, like it did in class when she was asked a question. "I can't think of anything," she whispered. "There's nothing I want to know."

"I bet there is." Kelly's voice was over-loud in the darkness. "Tell us who Jamie's going to marry."

To Jamie's horror, the glass started moving, pointing to letters that Kelly spelled out aloud, with satisfaction, "F–R–A–N–K–I–E."

And then the movement stopped.

"So, who's Frankie then?" Kelly asked.

"No idea," said Jamie. "Ry?"

"Nope, don't know anyone." They kept their fingers on the glass, waiting, but nothing happened.

It was Kelly who gave up first.

"I'm bored. It needs more people to work properly."

Jamie quickly moved to switch on the lights. "Disappointing," she agreed.

"Just what you'd expect." Ryan was smug.

Kelly turned on him. "What do you mean?"

"There's no ghosts, spirits – call them what you want – and if there were, they wouldn't spend their time answering girly questions."

"So how did the glass move?" Jamie asked him

"I'd have thought that was obvious."

"Did you push it?" Jamie could feel her temper rising at the thought of him making fun of her.

"No," he admitted.

"So, you're saying I did?" Kelly was indignant.

"I'm not saying anyone did it deliberately – I just don't believe in spirits"

"That's probably what made it stop working," Kelly told Jamie. "Anyway, I'm off. Better things to do."

Jamie winced as the door banged. She listened hard at the bottom of the stairs, but there wasn't even a whimper from the sleeping baby.

"So," Ryan asked her. "What do you think?"

"I'm sure you're right. Any of us might be moving the glass without even realising, and perhaps it's just a subconscious thing to try to make a word, or a name, like Frankie or whatever."

"You'd better look out for him though, just to be on the safe side."

Jamie ignored him. "But there's a lot of religions do believe in past lives and spirits."

"Fairy tales," said Ryan. "Anyone with any sense is an atheist. And it's time schools were atheist too."

"Ah," said Jamie. "Do you fancy something to eat? They always leave me a snack."

Despite Ryan's efforts over the next week to be charming, Kelly made it clear that he was not forgiven. Jamie listened to the casual insults flung his way and hid her smile beneath her dark curls. Every time she read the cards for Kelly, the other girl revealed a little more, surprising Jamie with the doubts that lay beneath the confidence she wore like armour.

Jamie knew that everything looked different from someone else's viewpoint, but she had never felt just how different it was, until she dealt the deck for her mother or Kelly. She had noticed their new Music teacher of course – they'd been relieved when the old one had stopped coming to school. "She'll be giving birth in the classroom any day now," had been one of the last comments. She'd certainly never thought about Kelly being miserable in Music; Kelly was miserable in most lessons. There was, however, a difference between being miserable because you were no good, and being miserable because you weren't allowed to show just how good you *were*.

YOUR SPIRIT GUIDE

SPIRITUALISM is the belief that the spirits of dead people contact the living. Its aim is to help people overcome their fear of death by hearing that the spirits are happy "on the other side" and to help people resolve matters that death left as unfinished business in a relationship. There was also the belief that the spirits could progress in their world, with the help and modern knowledge of living humans.

Spiritualism was very popular in Britain, the USA, and, to a lesser extent, Europe, in the 19th century when there were so many new inventions that anything seemed possible.

One famous spiritualist was Arthur Conan-Doyle, the writer who created Sherlock Holmes, the first detective to use forensic science. This seems odd but the curiosity of scientists, at a time when the human brain was a total mystery, made them explore such possibilities. Psychology had not been born and it was generally accepted that there was a God and an afterlife.

If you could press a switch and make light happen, or speak down a black bell along a wire to someone a thousand miles away, what was so weird about speaking to dead people? Scientists were keen to prove or disprove contact with spirits, using the latest technology, the camera, to record Mediums at work.

A MEDIUM is someone who claims to be in contact with the dead and to bring messages from them. The usual way was in a séance when a group of spiritualists would meet up with a Medium. they would sit round a table, hold hands in a circle and wait for the Medium's spirit guide to turn up. Sometimes this would be by the Medium going into a trance, speaking in a strange voice, acting out a scene; or perhaps weird shapes would appear in the room; or rapping noises would be heard and objects moved. Sometimes a glass turned upside down would move round letters placed in a circle and spell out words. This method developed into the Ouija board.

THE OUIJA BOARD

was probably named after the French and German for 'yes' (oui and ja), the board has a pointer, which used to be an upturned glass, the letters of the alphabet, the words 'yes' and 'no' and the numbers 1–10. Everyone sits round the board and puts one finger on the pointer.

WHO PUSHED THE POINTER?

When a question is asked, the spiritualist theory is that a spirit answers, pushing the pointer to create the response, or if nothing happens, that no spirit has appeared. Unbelievers would say someone is pushing with the finger on the glass — or no one is pushing and nothing happens.

NOT JUST LIFE AFTER DEATH, BUT WRITING BOOKS TOO!

Writer Emily Grant Hutchings claimed that Mark Twain had dictated a book to her, called Jap Herron, seven years after his death, communicating through a medium and a Ouija board. She published the book, but Twain's daughter later sued and the publisher withdrew it. Apparently, it wasn't even a very good book (whoever wrote it).

People were very keen to contact famous writers — imagine how much money you could make with a new play by Shakespeare!

HEARING VOICES MADE YOU RICH — IF THEY DIDN'T LOCK YOU UP

Famous scientists were popular too — think how much better your ideas would sound if you could start off "Einstein says we should..."

Jesus 'appeared' to more than one medium, so they claimed, to tell the 'true story of his life'.

GREAT FAKES

Some Mediums truly believed in their spirits, but even they would create an atmosphere, in a darkened room, with candles and hushed voices.

Other mediums deliberately cheated their customers. They set up their rooms so that flowers would suddenly drop onto the table, balls of light flash across the room, ghostly musical instruments appear and play by themselves, pencils write messages in the air or on folded paper in sealed envelopes...

Imagine what tricks you could get up to with phosphorescent paint, invisible wires on objects and furniture, concealed

drawers in boxes... with a tape-recorder (or the newly invented phonogram) you could make the most amazing noises or music appear from nowhere and some sexy outfits worked wonders in distracting the customers.

ARE THERE SPIRITS?

Believing something doesn't make it true.

People used to believe that:

* the sun died during a solar eclipse
* if you sailed too far you'd fall off the edge of the world
* being tied up in a deep bath for several hours cured mental illness

We still have a lot to find out about ourselves and our world. Beliefs change with knowledge.

There are people who believe that if a girl has sex standing up, she can't get pregnant; that doesn't make it true.

Don't mess with strong spirits!

Now that Jamie thought about it, she remembered Kelly singing in Music class without realising it, because there was music going on all around her, and just because that's what she did. What had the teacher said? "Kelly? Who do you think you are, Snow White?" and the class had laughed, everyone glad it wasn't him or her being picked on, and Kelly had gone quiet.

How much had that cost Kelly, going quiet? Jamie only had to remember the songs that poured out from her coal shed on the evenings the band practised, that voice taking to the air like a swallow in summer, and she had some idea how Kelly felt about singing.

And now something important was happening.

"He's seen me," Kelly was saying.

Jamie had lost the plot. "Well, of course he's seen you. He teaches us once a week."

"No, I mean at the club. With the band. And he says I have a great voice."

"But you know that. What difference does it make if some teacher notices?"

"He's different. He says he plays guitar with these other teachers."

"You watch yourself, girl," Jamie warned. And thought, *wear longer skirts*, but there was no point saying anything like that to Kelly.

Kelly shook her head. "No, it's nothing like that. He says I could learn guitar, try writing some of my own songs, learn proper breathing."

"What's wrong with your breathing?" Jamie asked. "Looks normal enough to me."

Ryan leaned across, no longer pretending he wasn't listening in. "I've been reading things about proper breathing. It helps singers."

Kelly bit back the habitual insult, unable to resist the bait. "Like what?"

"It's all to do with concentration. Indian gurus and Shaolin priests have different ways of doing it, but it's the same sort of meditation that allows you to control your breath. For a singer, that would let you choose where you breathe, round the – what do you call it?"

"Phrasing," Kelly told him. "I can read things too. Show me – and no funny stuff, mind."

"At first, I'll have to talk to you, and I'm going to use your back to help you concentrate, but then you'll be able to do it yourself after a while."

"OK," Kelly agreed cautiously, turning her back on Ryan.

"Kelly, I'm not sure this is such a good thing," Jamie started. "He gets these ideas…" but she knew just how far Kelly would go to be what she wanted to be, a singer. And, she thought ruefully, she knew just how far Ryan would go to be what *he* wanted to be, so she gave up.

Ryan touched Kelly's back just below her right shoulder blade and traced a big circle round her back, gradually spiraling inward,s and talking in a monotone all the time.

"Shut your eyes, and really concentrate on your own body and your own breathing. Keep taking as big a breath in as you can, now out, and, as I make the circle, you're breathing more and more deeply… in… and out, in… and out… then when I reach the centre, I'm going to pull the cord and cut your breath, and I want you to hold your breath for as long as you can.

I'm going inwards, inwards and – now!" Ryan reached the centre of his spiral, pushed a little bit more firmly but still with a light touch, and pulled his finger straight back, *like the school caretaker starting the lawnmower,* thought Jamie.

Her eyes shut, Kelly was still holding her breath as she crumpled into a faint, only just caught by Jamie, who cradled her down as gently as she could, onto the floor, tugging the little skirt into a semblance of respectability.

Jamie patted the white, unconscious face desperately, and wondered exactly where to find a pulse. Just as she was trying to remember the assembly talk from St John's Ambulance, something about 'recovery position', and a few initials to do with breathing, Kelly stirred.

"I suppose you could say that worked." Ryan contemplated

the supine girl with satisfaction. "Whatever it was."

"Prat," Jamie told him. "Get her some water. And give her some air, you lot. Pretend it's assembly and she'll throw up if you don't stand back."

That cleared some space round them, and Kelly was already looking at Jamie with the dazed expression usually seen in cartoon cats. She sipped from the bottle of water that Ryan brought back, objected violently to the idea of seeing a teacher, or even the nurse in the sick bay, and was back on her feet, if a little white and shaky, ready for afternoon school, when the bell went.

CHAPTER 12

Jamie didn't believe they'd escaped, until the train pulled out of Port Talbot Station, past the long, gray warehouse, the graffiti-covered walls and the back of a school. Ryan stashed their overnight bags on the shelf and sat down opposite her, pumping a small outbreath of dust from the maroon fabric that had once been plush.

The dust motes danced in the sunray, promising them a good weekend. The carriage was half-full, mostly commuters clocking off early on a Friday, heading back from Cardiff to Swansea.

"Change at Swansea," Jamie reminded Ryan. "What did you say to your Mum to talk her into it?"

"She has the times of our trains, including connections, your Gran's phone number, your home phone number – I swear she even has the phone number of the Kidwelly Fire Brigade, in case I get my head stuck in railings or something." Ryan shook his head in disbelief. "And yours?"

"Mum's not a problem – it's Dad – convinced the world is full of pedophiles. It didn't help when I told him I was too old to be pedophiled, or whatever the action is."

Jamie had no intention of telling her friend that her Dad had been even more unpleasant on the subject of 'that Ryan', turning her argument of being 'old enough' against her. It was only her mother's gentle reminder that Nan would keep an eye on them, that persuaded her Dad.

Ryan's thoughts returned to more important matters. "Auto-suggestion is interesting, isn't it?"

Following his 'success' with Kelly, Ryan had tried out the same pattern of touch and suggestion on a few more guinea-pigs.

The problem, as Jamie saw it, was that they were all trying it out on each other, and as she kept trying to tell Ryan, the 'game' was spreading round the yard like a S.T.D.

He just shrugged his shoulders, said the morons would always find idiotic things to do, and his job was to observe, note and analyse.

"I think," he mused, "that it's to do with whatever makes some people better subjects for hypnosis than others. And some," he glared at her, "totally useless."

To Jamie's relief, when she had given in and allowed Ryan to try his little hypnotic routine on her, nothing whatso-ever had happened. Bitterly disappointed, Ryan had cross-examined her, but all she could tell him was that he'd tickled her back, she'd breathed in and out, and no, she didn't feel remotely sick or faint.

"Perhaps next time?" he'd suggested, but, once was enough, she told him. She'd never fainted in her life, didn't see it as a desirable outcome, and was not going to take part in this particular experiment.

"Tight underwear," Jamie said.

Realising that he had not immediately taken her meaning, she clarified, "Like Victorian women wore, you know, corsets. When their servants laced them up, the women sometimes fainted, or during the day, just from being squeezed all the time."

He still didn't get it. "Holding your breath – perhaps it has the same effect whether you hold your breath or whether your breath is squeezed all the time. Then they had to have smelling salts to bring them round… wonder what was in smelling salts?"

"Have you thought of a career in Chemistry?"

"No. And before you ask, no, I haven't filled in the Careers form and I don't want to talk about school – this is a holiday."

"I suppose it's a theory, holding your breath. But I think I'm accessing hidden depths of the brain, which perhaps some people just don't have."

She didn't rise to the bait but looked out of the window as the train snaked past the back streets of Neath, then curved around the bay. They passed the new Morfa stadium, home to Swansea City Football Club, and terraced houses tumbled in muted ice-cream colours down the hillsides above the city. The connection was as easy as they'd been promised when they bought their tickets, the train for West Wales waiting for their arrival.

Past the industrial grays of Llanelli, the train hung over the sands as if aquaplaning, so close were the tracks to the beach. Although the tide was out, stretches of water shimmered by sandbanks, interrupting the illusion that you could walk across from Llanelli to the cockle beds of the Gower.

"Gobble you up, those sands will," her Nan had told Jamie when she was little, and she looked eagerly for signs of kids, lugworm-diggers or tourists about to be gobbled. No such luck, although every year there would be someone stranded by the tide. Further round the coast, fishing boats bobbed in Burry Port Harbour, bringing in the mackerel that her Nan had told her was good for shiny hair.

As they headed west, the scenery turned softer and greener on the landside, views opening and changing as each hill led into another valley, and then they reached Kidwelly, where her own Nan was waiting for them, with a smile and an embarrassing hug.

Jamie found it hard to slow her steps to those of her grandmother and found herself dawdling with Ryan to let her Nan catch up, then charging ahead again, until they reached the lane where Nan lived. Almost in the heart of the village, the little lane of about seven houses felt more like countryside, especially to a Port Talbot girl. The forbidding square frontage of the semi-detached rose straight from the lane, with no room for even a geranium pot, but from inside there was a panoramic view: across the lane and the hawthorn hedgerow, then a fallow field, as far as the castle, misty towers or stark silhouette, depending on the light.

Today the kind sun warmed the medieval stone into a backdrop for the cows that gazed nearby. Jamie imagined their black and white presence on the green pastureland that slipped into flood plain, bog and estuary behind the castle.

When she was little, her Nan had taken her walking round the muddy fields, horrifying her mother at the state of shoes and splattered trousers, and she remembered the breath of cows, loud, steaming, and the crunch of their flat teeth. Time was different here with her Nan, and she was suddenly shy, wondering what Ryan would make of it all.

She needn't have worried. He joined in the little ceremonies of Nan's life as if he were reading Freud. He followed Jamie as she collected all the fuss her Nan liked for 'proper table-laying' while the kitchen produced smells of baked apples and sausages frying, and the sound of a warbly soprano singing *Strangers in the Night.*

"What will we sing when we're grandparents?" Ryan wondered.

Jamie found it an embarrassing thought, in more ways than just their taste in music. "What will Kelly and Gareth sing?" They considered the output from the coal shed band.

Ryan shook his head. "It's just not possible. We won't get old."

"No," Jamie agreed.

The evening progressed at its own leisurely pace: eating, clearing up, a game of cards, Nan's favourite TV programmes – half of which she missed, while giving a running commentary on the characters and past history, so that Jamie and Ryan could keep up with the plot. Then there was time to talk, television gossip mixed with family news in a way that made you feel the two were the same thing.

"Do you believe in magic?" Jamie asked her grandmother, who gave no sign of thinking it an odd question.

"Oh, yes." She smiled at Ryan. "Not like one of those grannies in books, you understand, I'm no witch. It drives me round the bend the way a Welsh granny always has supernatural powers. It would save a lot of time if I had," she added wistfully.

"No, the sort of magic I believe in is far more ordinary and far more powerful. I remember as if it was yesterday, when Mark – that's your Dad," she told Jamie, as if Jamie didn't know, "came courting Laura.

He couldn't string two words together without falling over his own tongue, so shy he was, but stars in their eyes? There was magic there right enough, and you can see it in the photos. There," she eased out of her chair, picked up a framed photo from a small nest of tables and passed it to Ryan.

Unrecognizably young, Jamie's parents beamed at him, her mother in high-necked white, with lacy veil, and her father stiff in his suit, as if he couldn't bend arms, legs or neck.

"Every woman's beautiful on her wedding day," Nan nodded, "and if that isn't magic, I don't know what is."

Jamie thought of her mother's weary face, of what they hid from her Dad and his temper, of his nights at the pub, of the long working days, earning barely enough to get by.

"Not just that, though," Jamie objected, "there's more to life than getting married."

"Certainly is," her grandmother agreed comfortably. "There's rugby."

Jamie screwed her face up. "No," she said, "Not that story again, of 'when Llanelli beat the All Blacks and the pubs ran dry'."

"Goodness me, girl, that's the old days. No, I mean winning the *Six Nations*, and the *way* we won it – when it went right to the last game in the Millennium Stadium. Now *that* was pure magic. I wish your Grandad was here to see it. I know your Dad was in his element. And Gareth – he's not doing Sports Science for nothing. Are you a rugby fan?" she asked Ryan.

"Not really." The room was silent with disappointment.

"But I know what you mean," he tried to compensate. "I watched some basketball in the States, and the way the players moved–" he tailed off.

"American sports." Nan's tone did not encourage further contribution.

She sighed. "Times change but people don't. You'll find magic quick enough, the two of you – if you haven't already. Now let me show you where you're sleeping."

Bedtime was called in a friendly way, but firm and organised, and it was made clear to Jamie that when Ryan shut the trapdoor to his loft-extension bedroom, that was where he was expected to stay, and no visitors. That suited her fine, she thought, yawning. She would be out for the count all night, the way she felt after a week at school, or from card readings and Ryan's crazes. She was asleep before her head hit the pillow.

The wind whipped her hair across her face, long, waist-length hair, flowing freely over a blue gown that reached her ankles. There were shadowy figures around her but she couldn't make out any more than flickers as she paced back and forth over the courtyard, burning with anger, hating her father for what he had done.

Her mind battered against the news, refusing to accept it. He wouldn't, how could he, not his own guest, his best friend's son. But her father was indeed in London, drinking and listening to the King of England, whose armies, and coffers full of treasure, could threaten and buy a lesser man.

What if he thought this the only way to keep his people safe? Could he be trusted then, to hold one man's life as dear as she did? If Gruffydd ap Cynon had betrayed Rhys' son, it was the king's decision not the man's.

Her mind turned in its bitter circles yet again. Whose word did she have? Only Nest's, the Welsh wife of a Norman, 'all men's wife' so the joke went. Could someone who was true to no man, not even her own Norman husband, be trusted on this?

Yes, Jamie's reason answered, *oh yes.* Beautiful beyond, she might be, dallying where she chose – with king or warrior – that was Nest of Pembroke, but she used her power to protect her people. If not for her, the kingdom of Deheubarth would be in ruins already, but Nest had charmed a truce from her husband, and a peace, however uneasy, for the Welshmen of the south, her brothers included. And if Nest of Pembroke had sent hasty word to those same brothers, that they were betrayed, and by Gwenllian's own father, offering their heads to King Henry of England on a platter, then it was true.

"You must go, love," Jamie heard her own words, even though she knew that she was dreaming. "Wait at Aberdaron Head. There is a church there will give you sanctuary while I speak to my father, gain truth and, if needs be," her voice fell in shame, "plead your cause. My brother Owain will bring you word. He is with us. And if all else fails, the boat Nest sends can steal you from the headland, and keep you safe."

"Until we meet again, my princess." Jamie felt the words breathed in her ear, the soft brush of a man's mouth against her lips and he was gone, this presence that quickened her heartbeat. She clutched the token he had left, but, before she could gather her thoughts, the winds whipped wilder, stirring the mists into thick fog, whirling her to the gray scene she had come to know too well.

"No," she whispered, clutching empty space in her hand, feeling her hair no longer free but tight in braids, her armour and sword weighing her down, and so, too, the brave men who'd fought and died. How long could she hold off this time? She despaired, seeking, searching, drawn as always to the end of all hope, unable to hold out against the wild grief unleashed by the sight of Morgan's body, as she went flying to her own doom. "Cofiwch Gwenllian," she breathed, unable to break the cycle, feeling once more her arms pinioned behind her back, calling on all her strength yet another last time.

"Cofiwch Gwenllian!" she shouted.

Startled awake, Jamie tried to make sense of her dreams, which were becoming as circular and painful in her own life as the battlefield scene was for bloody Gwenllian, she thought bitterly.

It was easy to see where hating her Dad came in, even to imagine her brother helping her out, whatever old Welsh names it all got wrapped up in, but how the hell this boyfriend from Pembroke got into things, she had no idea. It wasn't as if she had any boys in mind.

Ryan… Frankie… her subconscious teased her as she drifted back to sleep.

When she finally woke again, bleary-eyed from what Ryan later diagnosed as the wrong sort of sleep, Jamie was shocked at how late it was. She bounded out of bed to the bathroom to wake herself with a shower, and was starting to feel more like herself, when she noticed the trail of black trickling down the plughole.

Balancing on one leg, she checked the other foot; absolutely filthy, as if she'd been cavorting barefoot round the fields. *Mad*, she thought, washing both feet carefully, and checking the route back to the bedroom in case someone had laid soot for her to walk over. No trace of anything odd, or even dusty. *In her Nan's house? As if!*

Jamie paused on the landing, hearing her grandmother's voice on the telephone.

"So, it's happened before?"

Pause while the person at the other end spoke.

"I don't care if it's only a couple of times, you should have told me, so I was prepared. She could have hurt herself."

Pause.

"I found the fridge door open and the cellar door open, but I don't think she went outside."

Pause. "And when it's happened before, you saw her, and she didn't realise anything, just went back to bed as if you weren't there?"

Pause. "I don't know, Laura, but I don't like it."

"Gift? Not what I'd call a gift!"

Pause.

"I'm not happy about this at all. I think you need to talk to her."

Long pause.

"Everyone gets down, Laura. You work hard, Mark works hard; perhaps you just need a break together. Things have changed. If you really feel you've missed out, there's still things you can do, now. I don't think age matters so much nowadays. Anyway, we can talk about this again another time."

Jamie recognised the clues that the conversation was ending and scooted quickly into her bedroom, to emerge innocently, a few minutes later, dressed and, as her Nan would say 'bright-eyed and bushy-tailed'.

Breakfast, which was not an option, was a civilised affair, with no mention of magic whatsoever. As soon as they were alone, Jamie told Ryan, "I think I've been sleepwalking."

CHAPTER 13

Once Ryan had stopped explaining to Jamie that she could be found innocent if she murdered someone while she was sleepwalking, she told him how she felt.

"I don't like feeling so helpless. My body could have gone anywhere, done anything – and no, don't start on about murder again, it's really not helping. I can understand why people talk about being 'possessed'. At least it's a way of explaining all of this weirdness."

"It is weird," Ryan admitted, "but that doesn't mean there's no rational explanation. It's all a way of acting out your problems, it's just that you're a bit more active than most people."

"Let's just forget it," Jamie told him. "I don't want to talk about sleepwalking any more, or dreams. Let's go look round the castle, get out of Nan's hair for a bit."

The spring sunshine warmed their bare arms as they walked the lanes to the castle, entering from the village side. Jamie rushed to the planks across where the old drawbridge used to be, so she could show Ryan the spiral staircases and the dungeons, but her friend called her back.

"Hey, look at this." Ryan had stopped by a circular slate sign set in a rough rock on a brick plinth. Reluctantly Jamie traced her steps back, noticing the date first of all, 1136, then the name of the person whose memorial this was – Gwenllian. "You didn't tell me your spirit guide was from Kidwelly."

"This doesn't make any sense. This is a hundred years before Gwenllian was born, and here it's talking about her dying. And there's nothing about Kidwelly in anything I found out."

There was something though, not from her research, but from her dreams. She just couldn't quite bring it back to mind. "We'll ask Nan when we go back. Forget it, come and explore."

It was not surprising if she felt as familiar with the castle as if she had once lived here, known every tapestry on the walls, sunk her expanding body into the luxury of a lady's bed, warmed her hands at the great fireplace. No, it was not surprising at all. Jamie had been visiting the castle since she was little and her imagination had peopled it long ago with knights and ladies, so these ghosts were old and comfortable company.

When their stomachs complained of hunger, they headed back to find ham sandwiches and apple juice waiting for them on the kitchen table. Nan's rings sparkled by the plates, and Jamie picked one up to have a closer look. When she was little she used to play with her Nan's jewelry and now she was older, it was family history.

She slipped them on her fingers: the wide battered band deepest, with tiny chips of sapphire that had been her great-grandmother's, and then the two rubies in their twist of gold. She held her hand out to admire the rings as the stones caught the light, and then she slipped them off, too big for her hands.

"Nan", she reminded her, and her grandmother eased the rings back onto her right hand. Even when making pastry, she never took off her wedding ring. "Part of me," she had once told Jamie.

Halfway through munching, Jamie remembered the plaque outside the castle. "What do you know about Gwenllian?" she asked her Nan.

"What everyone in Kidwelly knows," she answered. "There's the Gwenllian this and that everywhere, named after her: a hotel, a pub, the new village hall. Wait a bit, let me think. Well, of course you'll know about the battle, from school."

Jamie's heart thumped and Ryan's sandwich stopped in mid-air before he took another bite. "The one her father died in," Jamie offered.

"I wouldn't know about her father at all. No, this was Gwenllian's battle all right. 'The Warrior Princess', they call her."

"But I don't understand," Jamie broke in. "If she was

captured as a baby, and a prisoner in a convent all her life, how could she be a warrior."

Her grandmother laughed at her. "What *do* they teach you for History in school? Not that Gwenllian, the sad one, the last princess. No, our Princess was a wild one, all right. Caused the Normans no end of problems she and– now what was her husband's name again – I know – Gruffydd ap Rhys. You know what the 'ap' means, don't you?"

"Rhys' son." Jamie could still feel his breath in her ear.

"Well, Gwenllian was holed up in the woods while her husband was away finding allies from the north, when the message came that a Norman army was on its way from England to meet up with the Kidwelly Lord, Maurice of London – all Frenchies they were then, the English. Anyway, this Maurice planned to finish off Gwenllian and her family. So, Gwenllian being as she was, a fighter, she rallied her men and went to cut off the Norman army, giving her the advantage of surprise."

Jamie could see it all. "At Mynydd y Garreg," she said, "that's where the battle took place, near here." She turned to Ryan. "I knew I'd heard a Kidwelly name – that was it, Mynydd y Garreg."

She looked to her Nan again. "She was betrayed, wasn't she? There was a Welshman telling the Normans everything she planned, and they were already there, waiting for her, so the surprise was the other way round, and Gwenllian's army was outnumbered and down below their enemy, to make it worse."

"Well, yes," her Nan admitted. "But if you know the story, where's the point in me telling you?"

"It's coming back to me while you tell it. Please, Nan, please, go on."

"Well, as you say, the Normans were there but there was no easy battle for them. They say Gwenllian fought like a tiger." Jamie could feel once more the weight of her scabbard, the fine balance of the sword in her hand as she played the advantage of being left-handed.

"And she had two of her sons with her. One of them died defending her – I can never remember which of them died, and which of them was kept a prisoner. Was it Maelgwyn or Morgan that died?"

"Morgan," Jamie said quietly, an old Welsh lullaby running through her head.

Her Nan was exasperated. "Jamie, what is the point of me telling you this?"

"I won't say another word," Jamie promised. "Please, go on."

"Well then, the last straw was Maurice of London joining in the battle. He went upriver of the castle and caught the Welshmen between the devil and the deep blue sea."

In a pincer movement. Jamie nodded and held her tongue.

"And when her troops were finally defeated, beyond hope, Gwenllian gave the word of surrender, expecting honourable treatment." *Her hands pinioned, the unforgiveable orders, the soldier stepping forward with his sharpened blade.* "and they beheaded her, there on the field, in front of her men and her son. But she never stopped being a princess. She knew it was coming and she raised her head high and shouted, *Cofiwch Gwenllian!*"

Jamie's eyes filled, and she couldn't look at Ryan, who had stopped eating. "And we do, you know, we do remember her, with our hotel names and our little stone at the castle. She lived there for a few months you know, when the Welsh had won the castle and she was pregnant, she lived the life of a lady for a few months, but then the Normans were too strong and it was back to the woods for her, Gruffydd and the children."

"Can people go to the battlefield," Jamie asked?

"It's on a farm now, but I think you can go by there, if you're careful. They do say," Nan laughed. "that Gwenllian's ghost walks there, searching and searching for her head, and that she cannot be at peace until she finds it. I know you lot like a gory story–" Then she noticed that Jamie had turned white, little drops of sweat standing on her forehead. "Why Jamie love, whatever is the matter."

"Tell her," Ryan prompted. "Tell her," so Jamie did.

Once she started telling the story, it all poured out, not just about the dreams, but about her mother and Kelly and the cards, and she held nothing back.

"And I know there's a logical explanation for it all but I'm tired and I really, really can't face going to sleep into some nightmare where I'm looking for–" she could hardly say the words "–a dead person's head."

Her Nan's face had aged a decade while Jamie was talking. There was a long silence.

"I don't know what to say," her grandmother began, "but you're a good girl and this will all work out. You'll see. I won't tell you I believe in past lives and spirit guides and whatnot because I don't. We have all kinds of stories in our dreams…"

"That's what I say," Ryan beamed.

"But I'd like a little word with your Mum."

Jamie was horrified. "Please don't" she said, "I wasn't supposed to tell anyone and it'll only cause trouble, especially if Dad finds out."

Nan's face softened. "You can trust me," she said, and Jamie rather thought she could. She already felt better just for hearing all these weird things said aloud. If her Nan could listen to all this without having her locked up, perhaps Ryan was right, and there were reasons and sense behind things, even if they didn't understand it all. It was with these comforting thoughts that she went to bed that night.

She was still feeling soothed and protected when she found herself looking out across the murky waters of the Irish Sea, odd hairs escaping from their braids, whipped by the breeze as she shielded her eyes, scanning the waves.

Her brother Owain had already taken the reins of her horse, waiting with his handpicked warriors to make sure she was safe until the boat came – and then she would be out of Gwynedd's hands.

She shivered and pulled her rough cloak tighter, glad of her jerkin. They had nothing left to say, she and Owain, but it helped to have him by her side, to know that he and her mother approved this act of rebellion. She was not so lost in love that she had forgotten her duty to Gwynedd, to the very people her father said he was protecting.

She had listened to the reports, the mad Prince of the south with his dragon sons, waging woods warfare against the Normans, and every time her father raged, "We will pay for this, the fools, they cannot win," her head rebelled along with her heart.

Her father was the fool, tired and old. There could be no peace, not at the cost of friend and countryman, not at the cost of such a love. Then word from Nest had offered her the choice.

When she took Nest's words to them, her brother looked her straight in the eye and said, "We will fight again in Gwynedd"; her mother said, "Go to him,"; and here she was, awaiting Nest's boat and exile, skipping from foot to foot like a girl before Maytime.

"There," Owain pointed, and she saw the boat, bobbing on the waves. The sea was the colour of her father's tankard, the sky churning with rainclouds, and she was going to trust her life to the Pembroke sailors manning that collection of wooden planks. So be it. Her spirits soared with what she would later recognise as battle fever, with what would later be tempered by experience and closer acquaintance with death.

She clasped her brother tight, one last time.

He said, "Tell Gruffydd ap Rhys that Owain Gwynedd sends this seal of his bond, the finest warrior of our land, and may he guard her as his life or answer to her brother. God be with you, little sister."

Alone, Jamie walked down from the church of Aberdaron, the same that had offered sanctuary to her beloved Gruffydd six long weeks earlier, sanctuary less secure than Nest's boat, which was here once more, for her this time.

The boat seemed a toy, battling against the waves and then

the sand, as men dragged its trail up the beach, waiting to collect her. Two of the Pembroke men bowed to her, their accent strange as they called her Princess, offered a hand into the boat, pushed off from the beach. She would get to know this southern tongue, dear to her already, but she would not forget the harsh, hissing sound of home.

As the men ran the boat back to the water, jumped in and took up their oars, she looked back at the cliff, where Owain raised one mailed glove in salute, and then she turned resolutely to face her future. In the dim light, the red-gold of Gruffydd's token glowed on her finger, reminding her of his breath in her ear and her last words to him, "Never, it will never leave me. If ever I am parted from this, may God take you away from me."

The mists gathered, waves swelled, broke and fell, and still the whiteness thickened, dampened sound, blinded Jamie. She could see nothing, no one, and she was too afraid to put out a hand, not knowing what she would touch.

Worse, she thought, the sickness clumping in her stomach, knowing *exactly* what she might touch, where she was. *No, she screamed silently, not again, not here,* but the relentless mists cleared enough to show the mud, the sword gashes, the ravens. *I have no strength left, no hope.* She didn't even try to search, but drifted in the mist, drifted yet again into her doom.

When Jamie finally woke, she was tired but exhilarated. The sunlight through the curtains suggested that it was late enough to get up, and she rushed along the landing to knock on the loft trapdoor with the hooked stick left to open it.

Sleepy-eyed, Ryan looked down, like a stranded trapeze artist.

She yelled up at him, "It's not her head."

"Good," he said. "Is it morning?"

CHAPTER 14

"It all makes perfect sense," her Nan was saying. "I told you stories when you were little, then this Medium-person, whatsit–"

"Psychic," Jamie corrected automatically.

"–whatever, put Gwenllian into your head, and then dreams went as dreams do, all that mixing of what you feel and think. Why, I remember one dream..."

Jamie let her Nan's dreams drift over her while Ryan nodded enthusiastically, all attention, as he added to his collection. It didn't matter why or how, she thought, whether supernatural or psychological, her dreams had given her a job to do, and she had to at least try.

When there seemed to be a suitable break in her grandmother's reminiscences, Jamie said, "I'd like to see the battlefield."

This proved to be surprisingly easy. Jamie's grandmother drove them along some narrow lanes, bordered with hedgerows, and five minutes later they passed the sign for Gwenllian Farm. "That's where it was," Nan said. "I can't stop here but if I park in the farm entrance, you can walk back up the lane and look over the gate, and through the hedge.

"I'll stay in the car," she said as she parked, "just in case a farmer comes with a tractor or something."

Jamie and Ryan walked along the lane, peering through the thin hedgerows that were just starting to leaf. Hawthorn and blackthorn buds were ready to burst, the branches twisting through hazel and twining honeysuckle.

"It's no good," Jamie said, staring into the fields. "I need to get in there." They had walked out of sight of her grandmother, who looked all set for a snooze.

"Is this what you might call strictly legal?" Ryan asked.

"Maybe. Especially if we stay at the edges of the field. That's what Nan told me when I was little."

"And are we going to stay at the edges?"

Jamie grinned. "Shouldn't think so."

Then she disappeared through a gap in the hedge.

With some difficulty, gaining several burrs and twigs in the process, Ryan followed her. She crossed one field, stopped and took her bearings, lined up the slope and rocks.

"Yes," she said, "yes, this is it."

She felt the twists and trust of the horse beneath her, as much part of her as the sword flashing out. Like Saeth, her men would follow wherever she led them, but they wore no blinkers.

The snatched war council had aired regret for Gruffydd's absence, the men's doubts over how to deal with this new threat, but never a doubt over her leadership. She had proved herself too often in battle for that, and however much Gruffydd was missed now, it was not in her place, but at her side, that he was needed, by her most of all.

"To hell and back, my Lady," they told her.

And back, she prayed silently, *please God*.

The sheltering granite of Mynydd y Garreg rose up, just as Jamie remembered the black heathland, except of course it was green, so green. No mud, no bodies, and the little birds were singing sweetness and springtime, not scavenging among the dead. Colours and smells filled Jamie's senses. So, this was life, the baaing of newborn sheep, the freshness of grass.

Ryan broke into her trance. "You're the boss. Where do we start and what exactly are we looking for?"

"A ring. And I don't know where exactly but somewhere in this field."

"Should be easy then – not!"

They took different parts of the field and walked long rows, looking for anything shiny, occasionally misled by a glint of granite, even a bottle-top, but no trace of a ring.

Ryan gave up first, trudging across the springy turf to Jamie. "This isn't working," he said.

"But it's got to. We can't give up."

"Let's think first. Why did the ring fall off?"

Jamie pictured her grandmother's rings. "Perhaps it was too big for her."

"Then it would have fallen off years before."

"Wel,l perhaps she'd got skinny, gone bulimic or something, I don't know."

"Try thinking back, to how you were in your dreams. Was the ring on your finger at all?"

"How should I know," Jamie snapped at him. "I was wearing gloves."

He looked at her, waiting, as realisation dawned in her eyes.

"Mail gloves…for holding my sword, for fighting… so–"

"So it couldn't have fallen off your – sorry – Gwenllian's – hand in battle!" he completed triumphantly.

Ryan idly scratched the back of his neck, chafed by the cord that held his crystal in place, under his T-shirt. "So, where was it?" he mused.

"Perhaps I gave it to someone to look after, a trusted servant or something."

"Then it could be anywhere, perhaps not even on this field."

"It's here," said Jamie. "I know it."

"And you know you gave it to someone."

Jamie thought for a minute. "No, that's just an idea. I don't feel anything about it. But I would have put it safe, I know that. I don't know why I took it off at all."

"I do!" Ryan couldn't contain his excitement. "Why did

your Nan take off her rings?"

"To cook. I really don't think Gwenllian stopped to make a bacon sandwich for the army before she headed off to fight the bad guys."

"Not just to cook – I bet she takes them off to do the gardening, anything where the tools rub against your hand."

Jamie swept an imaginary sword out of a scabbard, felt the space on her left hand where her wedding ring usually lived, her token from Gruffydd.

"Tools," she agreed, "like a sword. You'd catch your ring in the chainmail, and you're a lefthander, so it's not like Nan – it's the ring on your left hand that catches." She became dejected again. "But that doesn't tell us where she put it."

"Let's check it through again, what we know. She took off the ring for safe-keeping."

"It was the most precious object she had."

"She fought, she lost, they cut her head off." Ryan instinctively stroked the back of his neck again, as if imagining the fall of a sword, cutting through flesh and bone, cutting through… His fingers lingered over a bump under the neck of his T-shirt.

"I've got it!" he announced. "You – she – didn't give it to someone else at all! She carried it with her through the battle, tied round her neck for safekeeping."

Jamie's eyes widened. "Next to my heart," she said.

"And when the executioner swung the sword, he cut through…"

"The leather. The ring must be there, on the ground where she was beheaded!"

"Can you find it?"

Jamie nodded. For the first time, she tried to find, instead of avoid, the place of Gwenllian's doom. She recalled the contours of the land, and she let her memories guide her feet until she felt the sickening lurch of old blood call her to the spot where there had once been a knot of people, and a princess about to die.

"Here," she told Ryan, and they scrabbled in the earth on hands and knees.

"We could come back with a metal detector," Ryan was saying, when Jamie shouted, "I've got it!" and held up a small object, dulled and muddy but with hints of metal showing.

Jamie spat on a hankie and wiped off the mud, revealing the old gold.

"Look," she showed him the endless loop engraved in the red-gold band, "a lovers' knot, like in lovespoons." She tucked the ring into her pocket. "We'd better go."

When Ryan opened the passenger door, Nan opened her eyes, blinking at them. "How did it go?" she asked them.

"Good." Jamie's eyes shone. "In fact–" She dipped into her pocket and found the hole through which the ring had disappeared. She turned the pocket inside out and showed Ryan, churning with disappointment.

"In fact," she finished bitterly, "I think we need to come back with a metal detector."

"Good God, is that the time?" Nan started the engine, glancing at Jamie as she climbed into the car. "How did you get your clothes in that state? And you going back home this afternoon too. I want both of you stripped, and those clothes washed and tumbled-dried, the minute these keys see my front door. Fine thanks I'll get from your Mum, if she sees you like that."

Jamie and Ryan were too depressed to say anything.

CHAPTER 15

Ryan came back from his weekly half-hour with Sam, glowing.

"I think he's getting somewhere."

"That's more than I am," was Jamie's gloomy reply.

Ryan ignored her. "And he's even getting interested in interpreting dreams. We had these really crap bible stories as a reader so I flicked through to find something gory – no luck – and we got stuck into Joseph's dream. Sam did keep saying "technicolour dreamcoat" but I've started him off on some more mature lines of thought. Predictably, the religious angle will be that 'dreams come from God', so they're all warnings or prophecies."

"Don't you think that's a bit heavy for a Year 7?"

Astonished at the thought, Ryan reflected a moment. "He's thick but he's got potential," he concluded. "And he's interested."

"Which is all you care about, someone else to bore silly. Glad things are going so well for you. If you hadn't seen the ring too, it would seem like just one more weird dream."

"Look, I know how you feel. We'll go back and find the ring but just shut up about it for now!"

"It could be anywhere!" Jamie moaned.

"At least we know that it is there, somewhere."

"I can't believe I was so stupid!"

"You were lucky enough to find it in the first place, so we'll find it again."

"I can't believe–" Jamie started off once more, and stopped when Ryan caught her eye. They were both distracted by the view through the classroom window. Swoops of pupils were converging on a corner of the yard, the magic word, "Scrap!" being passed unnecessarily from one to another.

Cool but curious, Jamie focused on the centre of the maelstrom where feet and fists were flying. One glimpse was enough. "I think you'd better take a look," she told Ryan.

"Oh, no," he groaned.

Jamie was not totally surprised that she was walking home alone after school that day. When Ryan received his summons to go to the Head's Office after school, she grimaced at him and wished him luck.

"But I don't know what I'm supposed to have done," he hissed at her.

"They'll think of something," she told him before they were hushed by the teacher.

There was no point hanging around alone so Jamie joined

the outrush at the end of the day. First out, as always in the last few weeks, was Kelly, but instead of following the herd to the school gate, Kelly dived back through the corridors, back into the Arts Block.

Jamie raised her hood against the drizzle. At least the rain had lost its chill, although the classrooms were freezing. All part of the inbuilt sadism of education; cook in winter, freeze in spring – no doubt excellent preparation for working in the Australian desert or at the North Pole, or of course in a Welsh school. Which reminded her, she really must fill in that Careers form.

The roar of a motorbike being over-revved at the school gate interrupted Jamie's thoughts. Some bloke, probably an ex-pupil, was giving the parked bike some throttle, his helmet hooked over the handlebars.

"Hey, Frankie," a boy behind Jamie yelled, and the biker gave some more throttle and waved. Jamie's heart thunked. *Frankie.*

Curious, she moved close enough to take a look, camouflaged by drizzle and the hooded gangs around her. The boy barged past her and exchanged a few words with the biker while Jamie dawdled along. The helmet was retrieved and the biker looked up, grinning at her as he caught Jamie glancing his way. She winced.

Looks shouldn't matter, she told herself, *but how could*

anyone be that ugly and live with it? Another session of revs, a wheelie and the biker roared off. Jamie stretched out an arm and grabbed the boy who'd been talking to him.

"Oy. Who was that?"

"My brother," was the proud reply. The boy was younger than Jamie but, as she and Ryan had discussed, the little ones showed no respect these days, not like when they'd started big school.

He smirked at her. "Why? If you're interested, I'll ask him for you?"

"Good God, no."

"Well, if you change your mind… he's called Wayne."

"I thought you called him Frankie?"

"Everyone calls him Frankie." He sighed at her being so slow. "Frankie, Frankenstein, like the monster, because he's so ugly, like."

"Frankenstein wasn't the monster, he was the inventor," Jamie responded automatically, releasing her grip and the conversation. "I mistook him for someone else… sorry."

"Yeah, right. Well, if you change your mind, let me know. He's on the lookout for a woman at the moment."

"I can believe you." Jamie put her hooded head down and walked home very quickly, jumping every time she heard odd revving noises or exhaust bangs from passing cars.

Ryan knocked.

"Come in."

Ryan's spirits dipped to sub-zero at the icy instruction. The Head nodded to an empty chair and he dropped onto its rigid plastic, aware of the four other people in the room.

The Head looked very much at home in the carved wooden chair, leather-upholstered, that served as the bardic throne in the School Eisteddfod. When he'd won the poetry prize, Ryan, or rather 'Myrddin', had sat in that chair, but that did not appear to be what the Head was thinking of now.

Nor was it likely to be on his mother's mind, as she motioned him to sit beside her, freezing the atmosphere even further, but saying nothing. Unbelievable! They'd called his mother in and he didn't even know what he'd done!

Sitting beside *his* mother, was Sam, who tried to catch Ryan's eye, with an apologetic smile. The effect of this was weakened by an eye half-closed from the swelling round it, and a cut cheek, purple as a split plum against the smooth brown of his skin.

An empty chair waited, hogging the silence, broken only by people clearing their throats in little coughs of embarrassment. Sam's mother was flicking at the copy of *The Afan*

Times she was holding, and the Head was looking at her watch again, when a firm knock came on the door, followed quickly by the unmistakably black hair of Mr Travis. Now Ryan was really confused.

"Really sorry to keep you waiting, Mrs Carter." Mr Travis flung the words in the air en route to the empty chair.

The Head's lips thinned further. "Now that we're all here, we can get started."

Sam's mother needed no further invitation. "Is that him?" she asked Sam, jerking her thumb at Ryan. Sam beamed at Ryan and nodded. "I don't know whose bright idea it was putting Sam with that thug but I don't send him to school to get weird ideas!" She shook *The Afan Times* in front of the Head, "and then when I come in to see you about it, I find him in this state." She pointed at Sam's grubby, torn shirt-sleeve, and he looked, if anything, even more pleased with himself.

Ryan could feel his own mother bristling and he wasn't surprised when the next comment came from his side.

"I have no idea what this is all about but if I've interrupted my afternoon's work to hear this woman insult my son, then it's about time someone told me what this is all about."

Me too, Mom – go for it, Ryan thought but had more sense than to even breathe audibly. Head down, was the rule in these situations, whatever you hadn't done – there was usually something that you had, and if you weren't careful, they'd get you for that as well as what you hadn't.

Mrs Sam turned her anger on Mrs Anderson. "My Sam's a good boy and I don't need some delinquent corrupting him!" She waved *The Afan Times* again, and Mr Travis looked distinctly queasy. "And we all know black boys don't do as well in school, so the last thing I need for my boy is some black 'mentor', turning him into the same useless loser his father was."

Ryan's resolve disappeared at the unfairness of the accusation, and before his brain could stop it, his mouth said, "Without me helping him, Sam's going to drop black boys' achievement in this school from 100% at C+ grades to 50%."

"Thank you, Ryan," Mrs Carter said dryly. "I don't think we need to get into statistical analysis by racial group, if you don't mind, but I'm glad you're taking your GCSEs seriously."

Her cool voice had cut across Ryan's mother, probably for the best, he thought, as he envisaged Sam's mother looking even more like her son with the impact of a right hook. It was a nice thought but.

The Head continued, "I really appreciate you coming in at such short notice, Mrs Anderson, and," she gave one of her very straight looks, "I know that you had arranged to see me about some concerns of your own, Mrs Wilkins, but I must point out that you son was in a serious fight today, and there are some facts I need to put in front of you."

"So, where's the boy who beat him up then?"

"I'll be seeing the other boy too, but I have to say he came off rather the worse physically," Sam beamed, "and he takes responsibility for starting it, so I think we can safely say that there will be no repetition of the incident, but," a look was enough to stop Mrs Anderson from doing more than open her mouth, "I think there are some explanations to give to you and Mrs Anderson, in front of your sons." Now she had everyone's attention.

"Sam's Head of Year can't be with us, but she has left a detailed report on the fight between Sam and another boy at lunchtime. Apparently, Sam has been asking other pupils to tell him their dreams, and then giving his ideas on what these dreams mean."

Oh, no, thought Ryan as Sam gave him the lop-sided smile.

"This," continued the Head, "has been popular with Sam's classmates until today, when, according to Paul, Sam told him that he was a 'Weedypuss who wanted sex with his mother.' This, Paul felt, justified jumping on Sam to 'sort him' but Sam fought back, and told Paul there was nothing wrong with being a Weedypuss as he was one too."

Suddenly no one, least of all Ryan, wanted to look at Sam's mother, whether Sam was a 'Weedypuss' or not.

"I think I can explain all this," chipped in Mr Travis, his voice a little shaky.

"Please do," the Head told him.

"The Afan Times–"

"See!" Mrs Wilkins brandished the newsletter. "I told you!"

Mr Travis ignored her "–has been carrying articles about dreams, and Ryan, who is one of our brightest pupils, wrote up research on Freudian interpretations, which Sam has perhaps not completely understood," he smiled kindly at Sam, "when he has tried to copy his mentor."

"Well I think it's disgusting, suggesting to young impressionable boys that they want – to do that, with their mothers."

The southern drawl of Ryan's mother made its ironic contribution. "Does your young impressionable boy read the toilet walls at all, Mrs Wilkins? Or watch the television news? Or is he selective in his corruption? Freud's ideas are hardly the cutting edge of provocative journalism but I'm delighted my son is trying to make people think!"

She would know about provocative journalism! thought Ryan, both pleased and insulted at his mother's support, anxious as to what she would come out with next. He exchanged looks with Sam. Could anyone be more embarrassing than your mother? He thought not, especially when it was his.

The Head cut in again. Ryan loved her. "According to Sam's Head of Year, Sam would not have been able to read *The*

Afan Times at all before the mentoring sessions that Ryan has done with him. He has come on so well that his schoolwork is improving generally – and Ryan volunteered to give up his time to help Sam." Ryan tried to look as if he had volunteered and was a kind, helpful, responsible person.

"He's been brilliant." Sam's one good eye shone.

Sam's mother looked unconvinced. "Well, that's as maybe, but I do think *this*," once more the offending newsletter was shaken, "is *wrong*."

The Head gave Mr Travis a significant look and he quickly spoke up. "I take full responsibility for that, Mrs Wilkins. I think you have a point, and that perhaps the content is too mature for some of our pupils, and I should have edited out anything… disturbing."

"Anything that mentions sex you mean?" *Oh no*, thought Ryan. Censorship was a personal issue for his mother, and sexual censorship even more personal.

Ryan cringed, but before his mother could continue, the Head cut in. "I've been very glad of the support of all my parents on our sex education programme but I'm sure we're all agreed that the school newspaper needs to consider its audience, and anything that Ryan can't publish there will find another outlet, perhaps in English lessons, Mr Travis?"

Enthusiastic nods. Anything to get him out of this, Ryan thought cynically. "There are more things on heaven and earth, eh?" was Mr Travis' helpful contribution.

"Are you happy with that, Mrs Wilkins? Is there anything else you want to say?" They all held their breath.

Sam's Mum looked confused. "Well I still don't think it's nice, what it says."

"No," the Head agreed, "Freud's ideas aren't nice at all, but Sam knows that now, don't you, Sam?"

"Yes, Miss." He'd improved in more than his reading, Ryan noted. "Can Ryan still be my mentor?"

"I'm sure you'd like to thank Ryan for all the time he's given to Sam?" the Head suggested, and the word, "Yes," dropped very quietly from Mrs Wilkins' lips.

Mrs Carter stood to shake hands with Sam's mother, which everyone understood to mean that Mrs Wilkins was supposed to go, so she did. Sam managed to hover by Ryan before leaving, just long enough for Ryan to whisper, "Write down Paul's dream for me," and get a thumbs-up from Sam.

When Sam and his mother had gone, Ryan stretched his legs out, starting to relax.

"Now," said the Head, "about the fortune-telling, the amateur psychology and this dangerous game where people hold their breath and faint."

As Ryan told Jamie later, it was like walking across a railway track safely and then being hit by an elephant.

CHAPTER 16

"So, I've promised to be mature, less obsessed with sex – more like the teachers…"

Jamie laughed. "And Travis was there. I bet you didn't say that."

"I just looked at him."

"No more fortune-telling, no dream analysis, no hypnosis attempts." Ryan sighed. "And I had some really good ideas for the patter, to try pendulum hypnosis." He put on a spooky voice. "You are getting sleepy."

Jamie knocked his hand away from in front of her face. "Cut it out. You know it doesn't work on me. And your Mum?"

"Amazing." He caught Jamie's sceptical glance. "No, I mean it – good-amazing for once. A two-hour lecture on freedom of speech, standing up for the rights of the press, a hundred personal histories of the time when she blahedy-blah, and then it was all over, in time for me to come round here."

"But what about the point of what we were doing? You know, the fortune-telling, the dreams, the supernatural?"

"Oh, she wasn't interested in what it was all about, just in whether we were allowed to write about it." Ryan shrugged.

"She's like that."

He thought back to the Head's Office. "But I'd rather have her than what Sam's got."

"Or what I've got, I expect."

Ryan was indignant. "I like your Mum. She makes me feel at home round here."

"You just like being ignored."

"There is that," he agreed. "No one's on your back here. Anyway, you said you thought it was working, you reading the cards for her."

"I guess. She's not spending the money any more now she's got me but–" how to explain the pull of the cards? She wondered who was asking for readings more now, her mother or Jamie herself? And then there were her own weird dreams and, now, Frankie.

Perhaps dashing around on a medieval horse was a symbol of her becoming a biker girl? There were a few things she didn't feel she could discuss with Ryan.

"But?" Ryan prompted.

"But she's still so addicted."

"I don't know what more we can do," Ryan admitted. "Hey, I'd better be going – sort out that History for tomorrow."

They were just saying, "See-yas," in the kitchen, accompanied by a television soap theme blaring from the sitting-room, when Gareth burst through the back door, dragging

Kelly behind him. She was struggling and trying to kick him, but quietened on seeing Ryan, who had the opposite effect on Gareth.

Diving towards Ryan, Gareth started shouting. "Think you can mess with my girlfriend you–"

Jamie didn't wait for the stream of incoherent swearwords to finish. It might be a few years since she'd play-tussled her big brother, but he didn't scare her, even if he was tamping mad.

While Ryan tried to hold Gareth at arms' length, Jamie tucked her head down and ran at him, catching him in the ribs and winding him. She kicked him for good measure, hard, in the shin, and then she started shouting. That was something she'd always been better at – he ran out of words too quickly.

"No one knows what you're on about, you stupid prat, so back off. If Kelly's seeing someone else–"

"I'm not!" Kelly said, tugging on Gareth's sleeve to make him listen.

"–I don't blame her! What she sees in you I don't know, you, you, you…!"

Gareth let go of Ryan so he could rub his calf.

"Bitch," he addressed his sister, breathing heavily but back in control of himself.

Ryan sat down at the kitchen table, defusing some of the

tension with his calm curiosity. "Getting to be a habit, this," he told Jamie. "So, what am I supposed to have done?"

Gareth spoke to Jamie, unable to look directly at Ryan. "Two weeks now, and she won't meet me straight from school any more, always hanging round there. Then, I just touch her back and she faints, and when she comes round, she's saying something about him," a jerk of the head in Ryan's direction, "helping her breathe or some such rubbish. I'll kill him!"

Between them, Kelly and Jamie held him back, while Ryan sparked, "I wasn't asking you, I was asking the lady."

"I've told him," Kelly joined in, her voice shaking, "I've told him I was with the Music teacher after school. Tell him, Jamie."

Light dawned. All that rushing out of class at the end of the day. "You great cretin! She's learning the guitar! Aren't you, Kelly?"

"I told him, but he wouldn't listen."

Looking for someone else to blame, Gareth turned on her. "So why didn't you tell me in the first place? Something to hide? What's he like, this Music teacher?"

"He's young and gorgeous," Jamie chipped in, eyes blazing, "but your girlfriend's too stupid to make the most of it."

"It was going to be a surprise," Kelly told him, "when I'd learned enough, I was going to play something for the band.

And we've been practising every day because I'm going to do something in school, for the parents."

None of them had noticed the television volume being turned up, then growing louder again as the connecting doors opened, and Jamie's Dad exploded into the room.

"What the hell's going on in here? Gareth? Jamie?"

The silence grew.

So did the epicentre of the earthquake, rumbling in Mr Williams" voice when he added, "Well, is one of you going to tell me?"

Still fuming and frustrated, Gareth launched in. "He's been messing with Kelly."

"It's a lie", "He hasn't," I haven't," the others cut across each other.

"I thought," Gareth glared at them as he amended his accusation, "he'd been going out with her but," he grew more confident, "he *has* been messing with her head, so she faints if you just touch her, and those two," he nodded at Ryan and Jamie, desperate to shift any blame, "have been getting Kelly involved with Ouija boards, and fortune-telling and weird stuff."

"No!" Jamie yelled, horrified, as her Dad's face darkened with the coming storm.

Jamie could feel her mother's gentle presence hovering anxiously at the door. How many times had her Mum calmed things down in the past?

"Gareth, don't," Jamie pleaded, but it was too late.

"Just ask Mum!" he yelled. "She even lets Jamie do fortune-telling with cards for her. You can't come into this house without hearing all that mumbo-jumbo about getting a better life, choosing July for a new lover–" his mocking tones stopped, as he realised what he'd said.

Jamie closed her eyes but she couldn't shut out the slam of her father's fist on the table, the crash of Ryan's chair as he jumped back. As if her father might have hit him, Jamie thought.

Her mother's quiet voice said, "Mark," and, as always, drew the fire. This time it was the door that took the flat of Dad's hand smacked into it.

"You stupid woman!" Everyone flinched and Gareth went white. "I might have guessed you had something to do with this. Work my backside off, I do, for this family, and I come home to a bunch of spoilt brats squabbling about nothing, and a wife that looks for romance in a pack of cards. Well you know where the romance went, girl," He turned and glared at Gareth and Jamie. "Just look at them. I need a drink." Another pair of doors shook on their hinges, and Jamie's Dad was gone.

No one could look at Mrs Williams. It was finally Gareth who broke the silence. "Mum? I didn't mean…"

"Why don't you take Kelly home," was the too-bright reply. Without another word, Gareth took Kelly's hand and the two of them left. Ryan took the hint and followed.

"I think I'll go to bed, dear, I've got a bit of a headache."

Her Mum left Jamie sitting in the kitchen, her head in her hands. "I wouldn't put up with it," she told the fridge.

It took Ryan ages to get to sleep, his brain scrambling like a hamster in a wheel around the problems of the day, while the rain beat down on the roof. His thoughts skidded from Jamie to school and round again. Was that what it was like to have a father?

He wondered, for the thousandth time, about the person behind the sperm that produced him. How could his mother not wonder too? Perhaps Freud had a point… *I must investigate Jung,* was Ryan's last thought before he finally drifted off.

As he usually slept like a hibernating bear, it came as a surprise to him to find himself awake again, and, according to his alarm clock, at 3am. What's more, he could half-remember a dream, the feelings of panic. He closed his eyes and concentrated, to recall it better.

Panic, someone drowning, someone… Jamie. His heart

banged. Jamie was in trouble. Of course she was, he rationalised, she was in trouble with her Dad, she was worried about her Mum, she'd kicked the fluff out of her brother. He smiled at the memory.

After a few minutes, the worry returned, and he couldn't shift the absolute conviction that Jamie was in trouble, no, not just in trouble, but in danger. *Mortal danger.*

Once the words had come into his mind, they lodged there, unshakeable. He thought about Jamie's Dad coming back from the pub, perhaps having a few words with Jamie. He remembered that fist coming down on the kitchen table.

Five minutes later, Ryan was creeping downstairs fully dressed, and closing the front door quietly behind him. He shivered in the lashing rain, but he just had to check she was OK, however melodramatic it seemed to be sneaking around the streets at night.

The street lamps streaked pinkish light through the rain, and Ryan loped the half-mile to Jamie's house. *Now what? Do what people always did in films.* He picked up some gravel in the yard and flung it up at Jamie's window, missing completely. The second time was a hit, and he waited. No response. Perhaps she was deeply asleep, in REM, he thought, having one of those dreams of hers.

He threw some more gravel and waited. Nothing. Just one more try and then he'd give up.

Third time lucky, he told himself, hitting the window at the same time as the sash was raised and an all-too-recognizable head and shoulders appeared.

"What the hell's going on?" yelled Jamie's Dad.

Had he got the room wrong? Fighting the adrenalin rush that encouraged him to run away very fast, Ryan stood his ground, calling up, "I just wanted to check that Jamie's all right, Mr Williams. I know it sounds stupid but–"

"She's fine," was the curt reply and Ryan thought he was lucky to get back something as polite as that, when there was a flurry of movement at the window.

"Laura," Mr Williams was yelling, "she's gone."

Then the window filled again with a man's outline. "Where's Jamie?"

"I don't know, Mr Williams. Isn't she there?"

"You'd better come in." And somehow Ryan found himself with Jamie's parents, trying to think where she might have run away to.

Everything blurred, taking forever, taking seconds, Mr Williams phoning the police, saying his daughter had disappeared from her bed. Yes, there had been an argument; no, she wasn't at a friend's; yes, he knew there was only one officer on night shift, but this was his daughter and no, she'd never done this before, and no, she wasn't the sort to look for attention; she might even be sleepwalking and he wanted them to take this seriously because, because… because it was his Jamie.

The phone was slammed down and Jamie's Dad held her Mum, saying, "It will be all right, Laura, it will be all right. Get me a torch and I'll find her. I won't let anything happen to her, I promise. I understand about the sleepwalking, I understand. Hush now. It's not your fault. If it's anyone's fault, it's mine. There's a lot we should have told each other, but it doesn't matter, nothing matters now, I'll find her. No, you stay here in case anyone phones."

Ryan didn't wait to be asked. He'd worked out that Gareth must have stopped over either at Kelly's or at some other friend's, so there was just Jamie's Dad – and himself. "Can you make that two torches, please, Mrs Williams, if you've got them."

Mr Williams just accepted the offer along with his torch, and the two of them walked out, into the driving rain, onto the empty streets of Port Talbot.

Jamie whirled her sword above her head, reining in Saeth as she yelled the battle cry of the Deheubarth, then allowed him his head as they charged the Normans. Old campaigners, she and Saeth, and many a time he'd saved her with a quick turn or the crush of hooves. *Boneddiges*, good breeding, the two of them, and whatever happened on this cursed field, their sons would live on, fine, sturdy Welsh stock. Her sons.

A mail fist squeezed Jamie's heart and the exhilaration faded, dragging her towards the horrors she didn't want to see, but she resisted the pull. There was something she had to do.

Saeth, she breathed, *old friend. Even in dreams, I can do this for you.*

She dismounted in one smooth jump, removed the horse's battle hood and tackle, dropped the saddle to the floor. *Run free, my beauty, along the sands of forever.* A snort, an acknowledgement from trusting brown eyes, and Saeth skittered sideways. As the horse galloped into the distance, Jamie felt the hoofbeats in her heart, quieter, quieter, then gone.

She was alone in the gray of battle, so much noise screaming in her head, pounding into migraine, and her heart empty. She was supposed to look for something, but she could no longer remember *what* for the clang of metal, scream of fighting.

The raven tipped its head on one side, looked at her, measuring her up. She didn't care.

"That was well done," said the raven. "Such a gift deserves another."

"Bran," she thought, recognising the mythical king.

And, as Jamie watched, the raven circled around the place where Saeth had reared and trampled the ground. It suddenly plunged, hopped a few steps, and stabbed the ground with its vicious beak, grabbing something shiny. Jamie felt sick, but looked anyway when the raven gave its raucous quark and dropped something at her feet, something she recognised, a glittering band of Welsh gold, with its engraving of a lovers' knot, and the broken leather strap still tied around it. The raven called its rough echo of cliffs and caves, then soared, catching a thermal to vanish like soot up a chimney.

The noise changed and, now, her head hurts with excitement, with love.

"It is very old," Gruffydd tells her. "They say the gold was mined here in the south, in the old days. Perhaps we will find gold again one day and our best jewel smiths will cover you in bracelets and anklets, my princess... my wife."

Jamie is wearing flowers in her hair and a blue gown, and there are a hundred people sitting in a castle courtyard, drinking. There has been a lot of drinking. Faces are flushed and men are singing, songs of maids and springtime, while girls are blushing, catching promises like posies.

She and Gruffydd do not need the drink, and have barely sipped from their goblets to raise a toast.

"To our children," he tells her, "and to our children's children, the ones you make up stories for."

She raises the goblet, sips, feels a flood of warmth. "My Mabinogi are not just children's tales, but for all to tell at the fireside on the long winters' evenings."

She turns her wedding ring to catch the light, the same ring he gave her as token when he left her father's palace, on her left hand now.

"I need no other jewels," she tells him. "This ring will always be our promise, one to the other."

The attention of the crowd has slipped away from them towards the juggler, and, of course, to the drink, and they are slipping into the shadows, slipping away to their chamber. Gruffydd stops her by the stairway.

"Would that this day – and night – could last forever, my Lady, and this be an everlasting present." He draws her into his arms, and Jamie feels a man's hands hold her close enough to feel his heartbeat. She feels his mouth on hers, but this time fiercer, sparking her own fiery response, melting her like quicksilver.

More, she thought, *more,* but a soft leather boot turfed her out of this body sweetness, and a husky voice told her "No", though not unkindly. "In your own time, little one. In your own time," she was told, and Jamie drifted alone through the skies in a chariot of clouds, like a cherub, high on love and goodwill to all men.

CHAPTER 17

Jamie's Dad walked so fast that even Ryan's long legs had to pump hard to keep up. The rain beat into their faces like fingernails flicking wet scratches into their skin, mocking, irritating but not stopping their attempt to get there first. Where, or before what, Ryan didn't know, but the feeling persisted.

They were more driven than the rain, and, if they could find Jamie by walking themselves to death in the rain, then that was what they were going to do. Every street blurred into the one before, a gray stone shimmer, windows glinting like malicious eyes.

Occasionally, Mr Williams would switch on the torch, shine it behind some wheelie bins or up an alley, but, increasingly, it seemed they were wasting their time for the sake of doing something, anything. Finally, they stopped, the wet tracks down their faces like tears at a funeral.

"It's no use." Until the words were spoken aloud, Ryan had somehow trusted to the adult to get them to Jamie. Now, the fear he had consigned to a tiny part of his brain for consideration 'later, when it was all over', spread through his veins like a paralysing poison. He knew, as surely as he knew Freud's first name, that Jamie was in mortal danger.

"We can't give up." He flung the words out into a gust of wind and Jamie's Dad leaned towards him to hear him.

"Do you have any idea where she might have gone?" Mr Williams knew the answer to a question he was asking for the third? fourth? hopeless time.

What was the point? They had stopped at a crossroads and, as far as Ryan was concerned, each road was as futile as the other three. They might as well go home and hope that the police, of whom there had been no sign, would find Jamie before anything happened.

He was sweating and shivering, too hot but freezing, especially his feet, as if he were walking these streets barefoot. He had a sudden image of that open back door, the one Jamie had walked through. She must have been sleepwalking or she'd have closed it. If she was sleepwalking, what was she wearing? Did sleepwalkers stop to put on shoes and coats? He thought not. He pictured her standing on the landing at her Nan's, wearing that teddy bear outfit she slept in, and he could see her, soaked through, stumbling along the streets.

He pictured her. And then he just *knew*.

"Yes," he said. "I think I might know where she is."

He had tried using his head and got nowhere. All he could follow was his instinct, the same feeling that had got him out of bed in the middle of the night, hurling gravel at a window. Mr Williams just gestured that he would follow, and Ryan fixed his imagination on that slight, girlish figure, in teddy bear PJs.

He tried not to think of all those failed experiments in telepathy. The closest they'd got to success was when Jamie had drawn a cat, and Ryan, in another room, had drawn a ball. She'd been disgusted that he hadn't drawn a cat just from guesswork, never mind telepathy, but they'd agreed that the shapes had something in common.

Where was she? He let his feet choose the way, trying to picture where she was, and getting nothing but noise, so much noise, the rain spraying from the heavy lorries pounding the motorway, even at this time in the morning.

What if? He started to half-run towards the small round-about that announced the sliproad up to the M4. With mixed relief and disappointment, he saw in the torchlight that the sliproad was empty, and he walked back down, followed by Jamie's Dad. They couldn't go up to the motorway itself, they'd have to leave that to the police, and it was counterproductive to think of the worst.

But there was something here… he really didn't want to walk away. Then it hit him; he'd checked one sliproad but what was there to stop a sleepwalker going up the exit slip instead of the entry? He ran around the roundabout, up the exit from Margam, and he knew she was there, before his torchlight hit the figure crouching.

She was turning over little bits of gravel and then walking a few more steps, nearly at the motorway itself, silhouetted every time vehicle headlights rushed past. Each passing car sprayed water, drenching her.

The noise was deafening but Ryan didn't have to speak, or even point. Jamie's Dad barged past Ryan, picked up his daughter as if she were a wayside flower, and returned with her cradled in his steelworker's arms. Did Ryan imagine that the rain tracks had deepened down Mr Williams' face?

The walk home was paced to leave the sleeping girl just that, still asleep. Ryan had tried to tell her Dad that it was dangerous to wake sleepwalkers but had been told sharply, "I know."

Jamie didn't even wake when her Dad lowered her gently into her own bed, brushed her cheek with his calloused hand and muttered to Ryan, "I don't know what you're doing in here – get yourself a towel and a hot drink from Laura in the kitchen."

The world still seemed blurred to Ryan, and he thought he'd never stop shivering as he allowed Mrs Williams to dry him and make him drink a steaming mug of hot chocolate.

She tended to her husband and cried again, Mr Williams phoned the police, and it was only then that Ryan thought vaguely of his own mother.

"Phone Mum," he muttered as he was pushed upstairs and

into Gareth's bed for whatever remained of the night.

Someone said, "I'll phone your Mum. Don't worry," and Ryan knew nothing more.

Jamie tried to make sense of what Ryan had told her, and she only had to look at her feet to know it must be true. Although clean now, the cuts and bruises made it clear enough that something weird had happened the night before.

Strange boy, Ryan. He was especially pleased when she told him how noisy the battlefield was, more so even than that the ring had been found. She hadn't, of course, told him all of her dream.

"I don't think I will get those dreams again," she told him. "There was something complete about it."

"Good. That means you've worked out whatever it was in real life, and you probably won't need to go sleepwalking either, which is definitely a good thing!"

"How can you be so sure?"

"I get feelings too, you know."

"Only if you've read the book first," she teased him. She was back in bed – cartoon cats on these PJs Ryan noted – and the two of them were off school for the day, with parental permission. Ryan had even been allowed to stay at Jamie's and to chat with her – as long as the bedroom door was left open.

"Ry," she started, then hesitated. "Do you think you could kiss me."

He shrugged. "OK."

He leaned over and she shut her eyes, felt his lips against hers. It was warm, and friendly, and disappointing. It was not how it was supposed to be. What if this was it?

I have kissed Gruffydd Prince of Deheubarth and I will never forget, she told herself. Ryan was doing something strange with his wrist round the back of her head. She opened her eyes and broke off the kiss. "Ry," she said. "What are you doing?"

He looked a bit sheepish. "Timing it. I was just checking my watch. Fifteen minutes – that's not bad for a first kiss."

"Not bad at all," she told him, "but… I don't think I'm ready for it yet." Did he look relieved?

But she *had* enjoyed cuddling him, despite something a bit sharp under his shirt. She prodded the sharp place on his chest, suspiciously. "What's that?"

Now he really did look furtive. "It's an experiment," he told her, "a crystal."

"No!" She hoiked the strap up from round his neck and pulled the crystal into view.

"It's a dragon's egg, and it's supposed to be good for my

aura, so I was just checking whether there was any differ-ence…of course, there isn't," he added hastily.

"It's pretty." She turned the little stone to catch the light. "but the idea of it having magic powers is stupid."

"Stupid," he agreed. He swallowed. "You can keep it if you like."

Her eyes glittered as she twirled the crystal, "OK. If it really means nothing to you."

"Nothing at all," he said, as he fastened the leather strap round her neck.

Back in school, nothing had changed.

"Jamie," Kelly asked. "Can you read the cards for me? I've got this performance in school and I'm wondering whether to go for this talent competition in Llanelli, a sort of *Pop Idol* thing, and I don't know whether I'd stand a chance."

Jamie was smooth. "Now, it all makes sense! I did a spread for you yesterday, and I couldn't work out what all these important events were, but it didn't surprise me at all how well you were going to do in them – go for it, girl."

When Kelly had skipped off, Ryan asked, "Did you?"

"No. No need," Jamie replied, and they both smiled. "We can campaign for votes when she gets on TV."

"You still reading for your Mum?"

"I'm teaching her to read for herself, for fun. I've even shown her some free reading sites online." Jamie shrugged. "But I don't know if that'll hook her. Things are better since she and Dad…"

"I know."

One conversation did give Jamie pause for thought. Ryan had been off chatting to some teacher about work when Sam came up to her.

"He's not here," she said.

"I know. It's you I want to talk to. I just don't know what to do, and I don't want to let Ryan down. Since he gave me the lessons and the crystal," Jamie smiled and nodded, "my reading's getting better all the time, and I've really really tried but it's not working."

"You're stuck on a book?" Jamie guessed.

"No, it's not me, it's him."

"So, tell me."

"Well, he wanted me to get all the kids to call him Frankie as a nickname, short for Frankenstein like, but I don't see why he wants to be called a monster's name–"

"It's not the monster it's the doctor who's called Frankenstein," Jamie chipped in automatically.

"What doctor?"

"Oh, never mind. And?" Jamie prompted.

"I told you. It's not working. Ryan just isn't a Frankie, and no one wants to call him that anyway."

"I can see that," Jamie soothed. "Well don't you worry. If I were you, I'd just forget about it, and I expect Ryan will too."

"It's not as if I didn't try – and I've got loads of friends since I had that scrap."

"I bet," Jamie responded, distracted, remembering that Ryan had been very keen to suggest someone had pushed the glass when they'd tried out the Ouija board. Would he? But that would mean… No, surely not. There was an extra spring in her step all the same, as she met up with her friend again.

"I've filled in that Careers form," she told him. "The dreams made up my mind."

"Executioner?" he guessed.

"I'm not telling you, but I'll give you a clue. I'm going to start martial arts classes."

"Kung Fu film star."

"Not saying."

"Maths teacher."

She laughed. Their new Maths teacher was having some difficulties settling in. "Guess again."

Jamie considered her mother's new holiday clothes a bit too sexy for someone her age but didn't say so when her Mum showed them off, asking if the cards were positive about love interest in the coming week.

"I would think so," was Jamie's dry response as her Dad whistled a tune in the bathroom.

"About the money…" her Mum said, "your Nan's helped me out a bit, so I can pay you back now. I'm thinking, maybe, about doing a course or something myself, and your Nan said she didn't see why she couldn't help me now seeing as I didn't cost them much when I was sixteen. I was thinking about what the cards said. Maybe it won't be this August I get more money, maybe it will take a bit longer, after I get some training."

"Mmmm." Weird to think of her mother doing a course. Jamie had never thought of her mother as being very bright, not in school ways. There was always a lot you didn't know about your parents, she thought, as she waved them off on what Nan called a second honeymoon. Best not to think about it.

It was different but comfortable going home to her Nan after school, even if Gareth was sulking because he thought they were old enough to be left on their own for a few days.

"You feeling better now, Jamie, love?" her Nan asked her.

"Much."

"It's when the magic goes, see. That's when the problems start."

"Yes," said Jamie.

ACKNOWLEDGEMENTS

With thanks to

the Ballyvourney Library Teen Book Club for their invaluable help with the 13th Sign edition: Art, Caitriona Donncha, Liam, Maebh and, of course, Kristin;

all those (too many to name) who run websites about star signs and fortune-telling; to Heather for going with me to a fortune tellers' jamboree; and to Martin for his invaluable pre-editing suggestions.

Gwenllian, the Welsh Warrior Princess, Peter Newton

IF YOU LIKED MY BOOK, PLEASE HELP OTHER READERS FIND IT BY WRITING A REVIEW.

THANK YOU.

You can contact me at *jeangill.com*

I love to hear from readers.

For exclusive offers and news of my books sign up at my website for my newsletter.

You can follow me on twitter: *@writerjeangill*

Find me on facebook: *facebook.com/writerjeangill/*

'Jean Gill has captured the innermost thoughts of this magnificent animal.'
LES INGHAM,
PYR INTERNATIONAL

SOMEONE TO
LOOK UP TO

a dog's search for love and understanding

JEAN GILL

FOR ALL ANIMAL-LOVERS

A dog's life in the south of France

From puppyhood, Sirius the Pyrenean Mountain Dog has been trying to understand his humans and train them with kindness.

How this led to their divorce he has no idea. More misunderstandings take Sirius to Death Row in an animal shelter, as a so-called dangerous dog learning survival tricks from the other inmates. During the twilight barking, he is shocked to hear his brother's voice but the bitter-sweet reunion is short-lived. Doggedly, Sirius keeps the faith. One day, his human will come.

"Jean Gill has captured the innermost thoughts of this magnificent animal." Les Ingham, Pyr International

By IPPY and Global Ebook Award Winner Jean Gill

ABOUT THE AUTHOR

I'm a Welsh writer and photographer living in the south of France with scruffy dogs, a Nikon D750 and a man. I taught English in Wales for many years and my claim to fame is that I was the first woman to be a secondary headteacher in Carmarthenshire. I'm mother or stepmother to five children so life has been pretty hectic.

I've published all kinds of books, both with conventional publishers and self-published. You'll find everything under my name from prize-winning poetry and novels, military history, translated books on dog training, to a cookery book on goat cheese. My work with top dog-trainer Michel Hasbrouck has taken me deep into the world of dogs with problems, and inspired one of my novels.

With Scottish parents, an English birthplace and French residence, I can usually support the winning team on most sporting occasions.